MURDER
SO HOT

MURDER
SO HOT

A Merry March Mystery

Eileen Curley Hammond

Twody Press

Cover designed by SelfPubBookCovers.com/ RLSather

This book is a work of fiction. Names, characters, places, and incidents
either are products of the author's imagination or are used fictitiously.
Any resemblance to actual persons, living or dead, events, or locales is
entirely coincidental.

Eileen Curley Hammond
Visit my website at www.eileencurleyhammond.com

Printed in the United States of America

First Printing: September 2020
Twody Press, West Jefferson OH

ISBN- 978-1-7325460-9-7
Library of Congress Control Number: 2020914569

AUTHOR'S NOTE

Thank you, readers. I hope you are enjoying Merry's journey, and I hope this book provides some respite from the challenging times in which we currently live.

My last book, *Murder So Deadly*, ended on a bit of a cliff-hanger, and this book begins where that one left off, so you may want to read it first.

I am so fortunate to have many friends who write and are willing to help me hone my stories. To that end, I'd like to thank Jenna Grinstead for being a sounding board, providing suggestions, and giving me such great advice. I'd also like to thank Eric Henderson for pointing out story inconsistencies and supplying overall valuable feedback. In addition, I genuinely appreciate the Buckeye Crime Writers group (especially the Board) for their prodding and cheerleading.

Any errors in the book are mine, and mine alone.

A big thank you to my editor, Lauren Pan, for her keen eye, visual sense, and pushing me to make the book as strong as it could be.

And thank you to my family, who has been an enormous support during the COVID crisis. To Caroline Silvey (Artist), who always gives great feedback on my covers and keeps my husband and me in stylish masks. To Kevin Curley (Playwright) for his weekly calls and encouragement, and to my brother, Patrick, who together with my sister, challenged me with fun online games.

Finally, I appreciate my husband, Robert. I wouldn't want to shelter-in-place with anyone else.

ALSO BY EILEEN CURLEY HAMMOND

Murder So Sinful
Murder So Festive
Murder So Heartless
Murder So Deadly

To My Curley Uncles: Jack, Tom, Kevin, and Jim, as well as my lovely Aunt Fran

CHAPTER 1

Jenny

I slid into the dove-gray, first-class seat. It had so much room, plus it had a built-in cushion for my head. And, there were slippers. Plush! I bounced up and turned so I could see the plane door. It hadn't shut yet. There was still a chance Mom could figure out I hadn't sent the ticket back to my dad, and if she did, she'd stop the plane if she could. My stomach churned, and I hunched over, pulled the pillow to my chest, and prayed. The plane door closed, and I took a deep breath. London, here I come.

First class was full, and everyone was so much older. They even looked older than Mom. Dad had booked me a window seat, so there was no one next to me. On the few trips Mom and I took, we were always squished in coach; this was much better. The plane departed, and I scrolled through the list of movies. It was so cool to have my own TV.

The flight attendant crouched next to me. "My name's Paul. Do you know how the seat works?"

I shook my head.

He handed me a remote. "Just press here, and the seat will move forward."

I pushed the button, and the seat extended. "Sweet! I can lie down." I pressed the remote and retracted the seat.

"Would you like something to drink?"

"A cola, please."

He went to the galley for my soda.

What a crazy week. So many times, I thought Mom would figure it out. First, she looked suspicious when she found me doing laundry. Then she almost caught my boyfriend, Jacob, when he came to get my suitcase. I shifted in the seat and chewed a fingernail. *She'll probably never forgive me. Maybe this was a mistake.*

Paul placed a soda on the tray along with a small dish of nuts. "Comfy? Dinner will be ready in another thirty minutes."

There was no sense worrying about how much trouble I was in until my mom could reach me. I popped a walnut in my mouth.

Paul tapped my shoulder.

I jumped. I'd fallen asleep.

"I don't mean to wake you, but would you like dinner?"

"Please."

He placed a shrimp cocktail in front of me. The next course was a filet of beef with scalloped potatoes, and dessert was a flourless chocolate cake.

I put my napkin down, and Paul picked up the tray. "May I get you another soda?"

"I'm stuffed, but maybe later. Everything was so good."

I pressed the seat recline button, pulled up the blanket, and stretched out. The TV played in the background as my eyes drooped.

The smell of coffee brewing woke me. I hopped up and made my way to the lavatory to brush my teeth and hair. Then, I wandered back to my seat. Paul brought me a croissant, scrambled eggs, and hot chocolate. As I ate, I wondered what my mom was doing. She was probably freaking out and was never going to forgive me. My stomach flipped, and I clenched the mug. Mom had enough problems without me adding to them.

The woman across the aisle asked, "Are you okay? You're very pale."

I plopped the mug down. "I'm fine, although I'll be happier when I land."

"Not much longer now." She picked her book back up.

I chewed my fingernail. It had been great to have Dad and Arianna living next door to Mom and me and to have the chance to get to know him again after his four long years in jail. But then he and Arianna left for Brunei. When he sent me the ticket to London, I had been so happy because I missed him.

It was unfair of Mom to say no to this trip. If she had said yes, I wouldn't have had to trick her. She was probably never going to trust me again. I sighed. The steward picked up the trays, and I stared out the window as the plane began to descend. As my mom would say, I made my bed, and now I'd have to lay in it.

The plane landed, and my spirits lifted. I joined the queue leaving the plane and then merged into the crowd heading for baggage claim. Everything was so clean and white. There was a blue stripe on either side of the corridor that seemed to go on for miles.

My hands began to sweat as I approached Immigration and Customs. Usually Mom handled this, and I didn't have to say anything. What if she told someone I was on the plane? Would they take me into custody? I backed up and stepped on someone's foot. He glared at me as he walked past to get in line. I took a deep breath, joined another line, and finally, it was my turn. The Immigration's official seemed to take a long time examining my passport, and just as I thought I was going to jump out of my skin, he handed it back and told me to have a good trip. I wiped my hands on my jeans.

Dad and Arianna stood in front of the M & S Food store, just where they told me to meet them. "Dad!"

He gave me a bear hug and took my suitcase. "I've missed you, smart stuff!"

Arianna stepped forward and hugged me. "It's good to see you, Jenny. Are you tired?"

"I slept on the plane. I can't wait to see London."

"Let's go. I have a driver circling, so he should be here soon." Dad led the way, with Arianna right behind.

I followed them to the curb. As soon as I stepped outside, it felt like a wet napkin shrouded my face. "Wow. It's not raining, but there's so much moisture in the air."

Arianna laughed. "Welcome to London."

"I need to turn on my phone." It buzzed non-stop.

Dad's eyebrow rose. "That's a lot of messages."

"I guess." My face heated up.

He lifted my chin. "What's wrong?"

"Nothing. I get lots of texts, and that was a long plane ride."

"Uh-huh." He continued to stare at me, and my face grew even hotter, like I had just stepped out of a sauna.

"I was surprised you were able to get your mom to change her mind because when she talked to me, she was adamant that she was not going to let you come."

"Is that the guy?" I pointed at a limo gliding to a stop near us.

"He can wait."

I looked to Arianna for help. She stood silent.

"Okay. Mom didn't exactly change her mind."

His eyebrow rose.

"I didn't tell her I was coming. I had Jacob take me to the plane."

He shrugged. "You're in London. Let's have fun until she gets here."

"You think she'll come?"

"I have no doubt."

Arianna took my hand. "Let's go. I have so much to show you. First, we'll stop by the house. Then we'll go shopping."

The driver stowed my suitcase in the "boot." Dad sat up front, and Arianna and I sat in the back. As the car drove from the airport, I told them all about the final weeks of school and the sports dinner, where

I'd won a trophy in basketball for best team player. Then, they shared stories of their life in Brunei.

Green rolling hills stretched before us, and I moved closer to the window. "What's this area called?"

Dad checked a map. "I think it's the Surrey Hills Area of Outstanding Beauty."

"It's pretty. I can't believe I'm in England." My face hurt from smiling so much.

We continued chatting, and then we passed a sign for Wimbledon. I jumped in my seat. "Wimbledon! Do you think we could get tickets?"

Arianna smiled. "Already taken care of, I have a friend."

"This trip is going to be great." I sat back as the car turned. The houses ahead were all different colors. "How pretty!"

"It's called Rainbow Row. It's fun, isn't it? Won't be long now."

The car pulled in front of a stately white house with a beautiful side garden ablaze in tea roses and dripping with lilac wisteria. The neighborhood looked far more expensive than the one where I lived. "Is this it? It's like the house in *Mary Poppins*. I love the iron railings on the top. And, that chimney—it's so big!"

Dad opened the car door. "Welcome home. Let's go on a quick tour, give you a few moments to get settled, and then we'll explore. Your bedroom is on the third floor."

We walked up the few steps, and he opened the front door. The floors were a creamy white marble with an enormous fireplace on the left side of the room. A vase with a tall assortment of vibrant flowers adorned the elegant mahogany table in the entryway. Muted floral sofas facing each other near the fireplace were just past the table. I sank onto one of them. "So pretty."

Arianna pointed toward the other end of the room. "Kitchen's in there. Let's go up to your room."

We climbed the stairs, pausing on the second floor. Dad said, "Our room's down this corridor." We continued up, and the stairs emptied to a large lounge complete with TV.

Arianna opened a door on the left, revealing a lovely room with an elevated queen bed. The comforter was starched white, and the bed looked like it had never been slept in. She continued and opened a door at the end of the room. "And, here's your bath."

A white claw-foot tub sat in front of the window looking onto the treed courtyard below. There were a separate shower and a large white pedestal sink. I spun around. "This is even better than Mom's bathroom!"

"Her bathroom is beautiful." Arianna chuckled. She had been in town when my mother had her bath remodeled earlier in the year. "We'll give you a few minutes to unpack, and then we'll be on our way."

My dad hugged me. "I'm glad you're here." He and Arianna shut the door behind them.

I flung myself on the bed. *Super comfy!*

I sighed. I might as well face the music. I pulled out my phone. There were five texts from Mom and two from Jacob. I sent him a quick text to let him know I'd arrived and then opened the first one from Mom. It was short: "I can't believe you went to London." The next one read: "You're grounded till you're thirty." And, the third: "If you don't send me your address the minute you land, I'll disown you." The next two were flame emojis.

I gulped and typed: "Sorry, Mom. Landed. Here's Dad's address. I'll call you soon." I put in the address, stared at my phone, and switched it off. I'd better not give her the chance to call me. I glanced at my suitcase but decided to leave unpacking till later. After a quick swipe of lip gloss, I ran downstairs.

Dad and Arianna waited by the entryway table, and Dad said, "Did you talk to your mom?"

"I sent her a text. We're good."

"Ready to go?"

"Yes!"

The rest of the day was like a dream. Arianna had gotten us fast track tickets on the London Eye so we wouldn't have to wait in line. The weather was crystal clear; we could see many of London's main attractions: Big Ben, Parliament, and Westminster Abbey.

After that, the car took us to Claridge's for afternoon tea. The lobby was beautiful with black and white gleaming checkerboard floors. The crystal chandeliers were epic. Dad ordered a mix of savory sandwiches, including my favorite, roast beef with brie on rye, as well as an assortment of beautifully decorated sweet pastries. After sampling one, I leaned back in my chair. "This is the best place I've ever been."

"I'm glad you're enjoying yourself." Arianna smiled. "After tea, I thought we'd have the driver take us to Harrods. We can walk this off and do a bit of shopping."

"That sounds great. What are we going to do after that?"

Dad laughed. "I think after all this, you'll be tired. We can call out for dinner when we get home; some good places deliver in Notting Hill."

"But I'm in London. I want to see everything!"

"We have plenty of time. Tomorrow, I thought we'd go to Buckingham Palace and see the changing of the guard. And, then later in the week, we have tickets to see Parliament and the Tower."

"I can't wait to see all the jewels." I popped another pastry in my mouth.

* * *

I yawned. "Best day of my life. Mom will flip over the sweater I bought her."

Dad kissed my forehead. "Go to bed. We'll get started bright and early tomorrow."

I ran up the stairs to my room, dropped my shopping bags and purse on the dresser, pulled out pajamas, and walked into the bathroom to brush my teeth. I debated turning on my phone to see if Jacob texted me, but decided it would be better not to see anything my mother had sent. I vaulted into bed and sank into the luxurious mattress. "Heaven."

✳ ✳ ✳

The Vikings were eight people strong on either side of the battering ram. They moved as one, and the large wooden implement traveled forward to hit the immense door. It vibrated but didn't break. They regrouped and tried again. This time the door splintered, and they rushed through, shouting. That was odd. Why would Vikings call out "police" as they advanced?

I sat straight up in bed and rubbed my eyes. People were yelling in the house, and it was hard to make out what they were saying. Climbing out of bed, I pulled a sweater over my pajamas, slipped my sneakers on, and poked my head out the door. I edged to the staircase and looked down. A policeman handcuffed my father and said, "You do not have to say anything. But, it may harm your defense if you do not mention when questioned something which you later rely on in court. Anything you do say may be given in evidence."

I ran down the stairs. "Where are you taking my father?"

The policeman studied me and then nodded to one of the policewomen. "She'll have to come with us."

"But I haven't showered, or even dressed." I pointed at my pajamas.

He motioned to the other officers. "Let's go."

One policeman led with Dad, another held Arianna's arm, and my escort and I brought up the rear. Just before the door, the policewoman grabbed a raincoat from the stand and threw it over top of me. Bright lights flashed, and cameras clicked. Someone pushed down on my head when we got to the car. I climbed in, and the officer sat next to me. I trembled as tears poured down my face. *Was I being arrested? My mom was right. I should have listened to her.*

CHAPTER 2

Rob

It was a tight fit, but somehow I squeezed myself into the middle seat on the plane. I shot one last text to Merry: "On plane. Back online when I arrive. Love you."

I pulled the neck pillow from the knapsack and put in my earbuds. As soon as the plane took off, I reclined my seat slightly and got settled. It was a good thing I had traveled rough as a reporter for so many years. Helicopters were the worst. I could do the middle seat, no problem.

Midway through the flight, I stood to stretch my legs and walked the length of economy. The curtain wasn't quite closed to first-class, and people were stretched out flat and sleeping. *How lucky.* I returned to my seat, opened a granola bar, and got as comfortable as I could. Why did Jenny go to London when she knew her mother was dead set against it? I sighed. Kids made mistakes all the time; I just hoped this one wouldn't cost her. And Merry, I hated to leave her behind.

The plane landed, and the aisle was stuffed with people trying to be the first one out the door. I turned on my phone. Three texts from Merry. I sent one back: "Landed will call from hotel."

I had carried on my bag, so most of the people from the plane ended up behind me in Immigration. The cab took me to the hotel, and I called Merry. "Got to the hotel. I plan to head over to Drew's at eight."

"Maybe you should go now."

"Merry, any way you look at it, this is not going to go well. It'll be worse if I wake everyone up. I booked Jenny and me on a flight out late today. I'll make sure she's on it. Try to get to sleep."

"The waiting is making me crazy."

"Hang in there. I'm going to try and get a few hours of sleep. I love you."

"Love you too. Thanks for doing this."

I hung up the phone, stripped down to my underwear, and slid into bed.

The phone alarm vibrated at six-thirty. I turned on the TV, put a pod in the Keurig, and hopped in the shower. After toweling off, I retrieved the coffee, stealing sips as I shaved. "Breaking News: In a joint FBI and Interpol raid this morning, American swindler Drew March, international fashion model Arianna Flores, and an unnamed accomplice were taken into custody."

I ran back into the bedroom just in time to catch a glimpse of three people being led from a house. *Crap.* I picked up my phone and called Merry. It rang and then went to voicemail. *She must have turned her phone off to get some sleep.*

The news continued, and I froze the screen. Could it be? Yes. My FBI pal Christina Patel. No time like the present to renew old acquaintances. I pulled up her number and texted: "In London. Need to see you ASAP."

"Kind of busy right now."

"I saw. Need to talk."

"One hour. Notting Hill police station."

"I'll be there."

I tossed the rest of the coffee down my throat, grabbed my knapsack, and walked out the door to the nearest Tube station. The trip took less time than I thought, so I arrived a few minutes early and alerted the person on the desk I was there. Ten minutes later, Christina walked toward me. Tall and trim, her gleaming straight black hair swung free. I stood and kissed her cheek. "You look terrific."

She smiled. "So do you, although I'm surprised to see you. What are you doing in London?"

"I was supposed to be retrieving my girlfriend's wayward daughter."

"Ooh. Girlfriend. Is it serious?"

"It is."

"That makes me feel less guilty about dumping you."

"And, how is Ravi?"

"The best. How long are you in town? We could have drinks." She pushed her hair over her shoulder. "It's great to see you, Rob, but I'm working a case. What's up?"

"I think you have my girlfriend's daughter, Jenny March. She arrived the day before yesterday, and I can assure you she has nothing to do with her father's shady dealings. She's only seventeen."

"That checks with our information. Since we're old friends, and as long as she verifies that her mother sent you, you can take her with you. She's down here." Christina led me through the bullpen to the interview rooms beyond. "This one."

I opened the door, and Jenny launched herself into my arms. "Mr. Jenson. I've never been so glad to see anyone in my life."

I hugged her. "Let's go home."

"What about my dad?"

"I have no doubt he'll be back in the United States before too long. Where's your stuff?"

"Still at the house."

I turned to Christina. "Can she get her belongings?"

"I'll ask one of the police to accompany you." She turned her attention to Jenny. "You'll need to identify everything that belongs to you and just to you."

A policewoman drove us back to the Notting Hill house and walked in with us. We were only allowed to go to Jenny's room on the third floor, and luckily, she hadn't unpacked. The policewoman did a quick search, and Jenny ducked into the bathroom to get dressed. Then she packed her toiletries and gifts, and I carried her suitcase down the stairs. The policewoman volunteered to drive us to Gatwick, but I assured her we could find our way on the Tube. We walked to the station and got onto the train. Jenny sank next to me. "It was like a nightmare."

"I'm sure it was."

"They came so early."

"It's a tactic they use to get people at their most vulnerable."

"That sucks." She leaned against my shoulder. "Thanks for coming to get me. Wait a minute. Where's Mom? Why isn't she here? Is she okay?"

"I'm sure she's fine. She had legal difficulties she needed to iron out, so I volunteered to come to get you."

Her eyebrow rose. "She was arrested?"

"I'm sure they'll have it all straightened out by the time we get home."

"She was in jail?"

"Just overnight."

"That's terrible. I spent a few hours at the police station. I can't imagine being there any longer. Where did Mom go to the bathroom? No. Don't tell me. I don't want to know." She shuddered.

The train stopped, and I signaled for Jenny to get off. "This is our stop."

The doors opened to an explosion of sound; so many different conversations intermingled with squeaky luggage wheels, and children crying. Jenny walked off the train and then waited for me. After immigration, we still had about an hour before the flight. I turned to Jenny. "Do you want to camp out at the gate? Or do you want to take a look at the shops?"

"I'd like to get Jacob some of those shortbread cookies."

As Jenny wandered through the shops, I tried Merry again. This time I went straight to voicemail. Her box was full. What was going on? I sent another text, but it was like sending something to the dead letter office—no answer. My shoulders tensed, and I began to worry. I sent another text with our arrival information.

They announced boarding for our flight, and Jenny joined me in line. "Did you reach Mom?"

"I'm not sure what's going on. Maybe her phone's on the fritz."

Jenny put her hand on my arm. "She's okay, isn't she?"

"I hope so."

* * *

The flight seemed to take forever because I was so worried about Merry. It wasn't like her to be out of touch, especially since she was concerned about Jenny. After we hurried off the plane, customs was backlogged. We finally got through, and no one was waiting for us. I tried calling Merry's phone again. It went straight to voicemail. I clenched my teeth. *Surely nothing had happened.*

"Is Mom waiting for us outside?"

"I'm not sure where she is. Let's keep moving and grab a cab." We got into the taxi line and inched our way toward the front. I told the guy, "Hopeful."

He whistled. "That's going to be expensive."

"I know."

The driver loaded the luggage in the trunk, and Jenny and I climbed in back. She stretched her legs. "Those seats were kind of squished together. It must be even worse for you; you're taller."

I nodded and ground my teeth. I didn't want Jenny to figure out how concerned I was.

"I'm so worried about Mom. I thought she'd be blowing up my phone." She showed me the screen. The last call was from the day before. "I'm going to text Cindy and see if she knows anything." Her head bent over the phone, and her thumbs flew.

The phone binged. Jenny shared the screen: "Your mom and mine okay. Just shaken up."

Jenny's face paled. "What does she mean? What happened?" Her thumbs danced across the keyboard again.

An ellipsis appeared. "Come on, Cindy. Type faster."

Her message popped into view. "Almost killed, but weren't. Both fine and at home. Too long for text. Everything okay. Your house is spotless."

"Mom's a cleaning addict. That's stupid."

I patted her hand. "Jenny, they're both okay, and they're at home. That's all we need to know for now. I'm sure your mother will explain everything when we get there." I was so relieved to know she was okay. My neck and shoulders had been as stiff as a board for the whole flight as I had imagined the worst. More relaxed, I sank back in the seat and closed my eyes. The sleep that eluded me on the plane crept in. It seemed like only a minute later when Jenny shook my arm.

"Wake up. We're nearly there."

The car pulled in front of the house. Men in white hazmat gear appeared to be breaking down some type of white tent in the neighbor's yard. Jenny hopped out of the car and raced for the door. I threw cash at the driver, grabbed her suitcase, and followed. The door banged open, and Merry ran out. "I'm so mad at you, I could scream." She pulled Jenny close. "Don't ever do that to me again."

I dropped Jenny's suitcase and my bag and waited. Merry turned to me, and I gathered her to me for a mighty hug. I whispered, "You had me so scared. What happened?"

She pulled away. "We caught the killer. That's what happened. Let's go inside, and I'll tell you all about it."

CHAPTER 3

Merry

The next morning, Jenny and I were in the kitchen. She sat at the island. "It was scary, Mom. All those police breaking into Dad's house and arresting him. What would have happened if Mr. Jenson hadn't come?"

I put the English muffins in the toaster and handed her orange juice. "You're lucky Rob loves us. Not many people would traipse overseas on a moment's notice to rescue you."

"I'm serious. What would have happened to me?"

I placed the butter dish on the island and sat next to her. "I don't know. You're only 17, so you're still legally a child. They probably wouldn't have been able to release you without someone coming to claim you."

"But, I don't know anyone other than Dad and Arianna there."

"Then, they might have put you with their version of Child Protective Services."

"With strangers?" Her eyes widened. "I wouldn't have wanted to be with people I don't know in a different country."

The toaster popped. I used wooden tongs to retrieve the English muffins as I figured how to respond. I took my time as I put them on a plate and handed her one. "Jenny, that's why I didn't want you to go. I knew something bad would happen. Something bad always happens around your dad."

"It wasn't his fault!" She stood.

"Sit down. We need to have this conversation." I buttered a muffin and slathered it with orange marmalade. "Your dad has an expansive view of right and wrong that most people wouldn't agree with, including me. He ran afoul of the law again, and now he's going to have to pay the price. The U.S. is trying to extradite him, and you know that when he returns, there's likely to be a lot of publicity."

"Maybe it'll be different this time." Jenny bit into her English muffin.

"Doubt it." I sipped my tea.

She ducked her head. "I'm glad Mr. Jenson came. Thanks for sending him."

"He chose to go. Remember that. And, regardless of what your father did, we need to talk about what you did. You lied to me. You said you sent the ticket back, and you didn't. Plus, you pulled Jacob into this. I've already talked with his mother, and she's grounding him."

Jenny's face reddened as she rose. "You didn't—why would you get Jacob into trouble? He was just helping me."

"His mother and I agreed it was a bad decision on his part. Now, as for you, you're grounded for a month. But, don't worry, I have plenty of chores lined up to keep you busy. There's a list you can get started on right here."

Jenny snatched the list from my hand and raced from the room. A door slammed a minute later.

I shook two antacids into my hand and tossed them into my mouth.

* * *

Later that night, Rob and I sat in the backyard, enjoying a glass of wine. I held up my glass for a toast. "To the best friend anyone could have. Thanks for saving my daughter." I kissed him.

18

"None the worse for wear. Glad to help."

"You must be tired."

He stretched. "A little. This won't be a late night."

I sipped the wine. The peonies were blooming and perfumed the air with an almost rose-like scent.

My best friend Patty's head appeared over the garden gate. "Private party, or can anyone join?"

Rob waved her in. "I'll get another glass."

Patty sat on the other side of me. "How's Jenny?"

"Right now?" My head tilted. "Probably madder at me than I am at her, but the good news is the laundry's done. Then, I have her painting my office. The house is going to look great by the end of the month, and, hopefully, we'll have mended our differences."

Rob returned and poured Patty a glass of wine. "To what do we owe the pleasure?"

"James, Patrick's half-brother, is coming to town for a few days to meet us. We'd like you to have dinner with us Thursday night."

"Are you sure Patrick doesn't want him all to himself?"

Patty chuckled. "James is getting here early that day. I think Patrick wants a buffer lined up in case he needs it."

CHAPTER 4

Patrick

I had pulled the drape aside for the fourth or fifth time when Patty said, "He's not supposed to be here for another fifteen minutes."

My chin jutted. "He could be early."

"I know you're excited, honey, but you should finish your breakfast."

"I'm not hungry. How would you feel if you had been an only child your whole life, and you suddenly discovered you had a brother?"

She filled her coffee mug and sat down next to me. "How you feel is more important."

"Happy, I guess, but a little scared too. James and I have talked a few times on the phone, but it's not the same thing as meeting in person." I took Patty's hand. "What if he doesn't like me?"

"He's going to love you. And, if I'm not mistaken, a car just pulled in."

I yanked the drape and peered out. "He's here." I squeezed Patty's hand and stood. "Let's go."

I opened the door as James got out of the car. He was tall, maybe six feet-one, with wavy light-brown hair and Cognac-colored eyes. He wore faded blue jeans with a deep-purple polo shirt. I gripped his hand. "I'm glad to meet you in person."

He gave me a sardonic grin and pulled me close. "I can't wait to get to know you better."

"James, thanks for coming. I'm Patrick's wife, Patty." She held out her hand.

"Pleasure." He shook it.

I extended my arm toward the door. "Come in. Would you like some coffee or tea?"

"Coffee, high-test, if possible, I had an early morning."

We walked into the kitchen where Patty put cream and sugar on the table, and I poured James a cup of coffee and topped ours off. "You had business?"

"I'm in sales for a technology security company, so we have clients all over the U.S. It was luck, and maybe a little surreptitious planning, that led me to your door." He winked.

Patty smiled. "Brothers, and you're both in sales."

"A smooth-talking family." James laughed and sipped his coffee. "It's pretty quiet here. I thought you had four kids."

"Band camp. They'll be back in an hour or so, and the noise level will ratchet." Patty lifted her phone. "Scoot your seats closer; I want to get a picture." Chairs squeaked as we obliged. She pressed the button and studied the photo. "I can see the similarities. Strong jawline, slight dimples, different color eyes..." She put the phone down. "I might have pegged you as related."

"Since he's pretty good looking, I'll take that as a compliment." I turned to James. "Patty's an interior designer, so she has a good eye."

James nodded at Patty. "You and Helen would get along then. She has a great design sense; her place in Phoenix is beautiful."

Helen. My birth mother. I pushed my coffee cup away. "You gave me a few details when we were on the phone."

"She's older. Eighty-five but still sharp. I know you want to see her, but I'm worried about what the shock might do to her." He lifted a blueberry muffin from the plate and pulled the top off.

I squirmed. "I know. You mentioned that before. I don't want to shock her, but I want to meet her. I want to know what happened. Why she gave me up for adoption."

"She wasn't married. Back then, plenty of people gave up the children they had out of wedlock." James broke off a piece of the muffin top and popped it in his mouth.

Patty's mouth dropped. "James, that's a bit harsh."

"True, though."

"But she and my father eventually married." My stomach churned. I stood, retrieved a glass, and filled it at the faucet, then held the cold water against my cheek.

"Can we back up a minute? I've heard various pieces of this story, and I'm still a bit confused. James, can you fill me in?" Patty sipped her coffee.

"Bro, you okay?" James asked.

I waved my hand for him to continue.

"I got more information from my mother since we spoke. My mother and our dad—" James pointed to me and back to himself, "— were married. A few years later, Helen started working for the same company Dad did, and they had an affair. Helen became pregnant, had Patrick, and gave him up for adoption.

"Mom said she knew about it at the time, but Dad told her it was just a one-night stand kind of thing, and she ended up forgiving him. A few months later, Mom became pregnant with me, and I guess they were happy. I don't remember them fighting much. That's why it was such a surprise when he left Mom for Helen. I was eight at the time. Mom never remarried, and she's still pretty bitter about it. I can't blame her; Dad swore up and down that he had broken it off with Helen. He lied." James sat back in his chair and began to peel the wrapper from the muffin. "It was difficult for both of us."

I sat next to James. "I'm sorry you went through that."

He crumpled the wrapper. "It's okay. I've gotten past it, sort of." He flashed me a rueful grin. "Got a brother I didn't know I had out of the deal."

Loud high voices echoed the hallway from the front of the house, and small feet thundered to the kitchen. "Is Uncle James here?" The oldest boy, Shawn, rounded the corner first. He stood in front of James. "Why aren't your eyes blue—my dad's eyes are blue."

The other boys peered around Shawn, suddenly shy.

James laughed. "Your dad had a different mother. But we're probably more alike than not."

I wonder if that's true. The kids clamoring over their uncle gave me a chance to catch my breath. I took a gulp of water.

＊ ＊ ＊

Patty put the various dishes she had prepared for dinner on the island so that everyone could serve themselves. Merry, Rob, and Jenny joined us.

"It's a shame Cindy is visiting your parents, Patty." Merry cut a small piece of lasagna and lifted it onto her plate.

"Couldn't be helped. Mom bought tickets to that play six months ago."

James piled salad on his dish. "My fault. I should have given you more notice. I'll get to meet her next time."

With laden plates, we made our way into the dining room. I poured wine, while Patty made sure the kids had milk, and everyone's water glasses were full.

"Since this is a special dinner, couldn't we have soda?" Shawn wheedled.

I tapped him on the head. "Nice try, bud, but not happening."

"When was the last time you saw your step-mother, James?" Merry sipped wine.

He sat back in his chair. "Last November. Since Dad died, I try to go at least once a year. I feel bad for her being all alone down there."

"Surely she has friends," Patty said.

"She was very active in the community when Dad was alive; they held all kinds of fundraisers. Now she has a few close friends and only does a few of the larger galas."

Rob reached for a roll. "It's sad that her life has narrowed."

"Her choice." James shook his head. "Hope I don't go that route."

"It's nice you became close and still see her." Merry leaned forward.

"She was married to my father for over twenty years. I visited them when school let out. My mom didn't like it, but it was part of the custody agreement. When I got older, visit times dwindled to once a year, usually at Thanksgiving. I still go in November, but it's the week before. My mom would go nuts if I missed out on her spread and didn't bring the grandchildren."

"How many kids do you have?" Rob asked.

"Three. They live with their mother, but I try and spend as much time with them as I can."

* * *

The next morning, Patty left to meet with a client, and James and I got the kids off to band camp. I poured coffee, and we sat opposite each other at the round wooden table.

"I like this table." James traced one of the divots.

"It's seen some service."

James tilted his ear toward it. "It speaks of a happy home full of children making memories and making their mark on the world."

"Or at least on the table." I laughed.

"Your family seems happy. Tell me about your adoptive parents and what life was like for you growing up."

"I had a good childhood. My dad was pretty strict, but I wasn't the easiest child, so maybe he overcompensated. He passed away a few years ago. Mom's still alive, and we see her as often as we can. I'm blessed."

"I'm a little jealous. Happy childhood, happy family here. Divorce for me, and you know about what happened when I was a kid." James paused and sipped coffee. "Makes me wonder why you want to see Helen. She didn't want you then, what makes you think she wants you now? Back then, they had closed adoptions for a reason—she didn't care about where you were and didn't try to find you. Why open that can of worms?"

I put the mug in the sink and rinsed it, staring at the backyard. Why did I want to meet Helen? My birth mother encouraged me to meet her, but what if Helen had no regrets about giving me up. What if James was right? But Helen wasn't young. What if she died before I reached out—then I would never know how she felt about me. I put the mug down and turned. "I've made a decision. I'm going to meet Helen as soon as I can get away from work. I'd like it to be a surprise, so please don't tell her."

CHAPTER 5

Merry—A Few Weeks Later

Things were finally beginning to return to normal. Jenny's and my relationship was still a bit strained, but we were working through it. Hopefully, by the time we went on college trips in August, we'd be done tiptoeing around each other. I blew on my coffee and strolled through the door to sit outside. My two cats, Courvoisier and Drambuie, wound about my feet as I walked. It was warm but pleasant enough to enjoy the early morning. I sat, turning my face toward the sun.

The bird song was rent by the obnoxious beeping of a truck backing up. I stood. The new neighbors must be here. The picnic basket I had filled earlier that morning with non-refrigerated food, paper plates, plastic knives and forks, and soft drinks sat next to my chair. I lifted it, used my hip to open the back gate, and walked over to introduce myself. Various people were running in and out of the house with boxes, and it was hard to tell who the owners were. I saw a woman standing to one side and decided to approach her. I held out my hand. "Welcome to the neighborhood. I'm Merry March, and I live next door."

The woman's skin was ebony, and she had gorgeous dark brown eyes. "Jada Jenkins." She pointed to a man helping carry a sofa. "That's my husband, DeShawn. Our daughter, Imani, is around here somewhere. She's sixteen."

"If my daughter, Jenny, ever gets up, I'll send her over. She's seventeen." I handed Jada the basket. "I don't want to get in the way, but I packed a few things that might be helpful to you. I know finding things after a move can be tough."

Jada smiled, and then one of the movers trod past, balancing an end table and some books in his hands. She called, "That's an antique—be careful with it!"

Two more people strode by carrying an overstuffed sofa. "That goes in the front living room."

"Thanks for the basket." She waved and hurried after them.

I told her retreating back, "If you need anything, just stop by."

She ran up the stairs.

I opened the gate to my backyard, sat in a chair, and watched the flurry of activity from over the fence.

Patty's head appeared over the gate. "Want company?"

"Of course."

"Your new neighbors seem nice. I met them when they were looking at the house."

"I'll chalk that up to you being a busybody."

She sank onto the seat next to me, pulled a scrunchie out of her pocket, and swept her long brown hair into an impromptu bun. "Hot one today."

"Iced tea?"

"Love some."

I returned my coffee mug to the house, filled two glasses with ice, and poured the tea. I strode down the steps and handed Patty one of the drinks. "Watching all the work going on next door makes me tired."

"They look organized. Jada told me this is their tenth move since Imani was born."

"Ten moves in sixteen years? That's a lot." I shifted in the chair. "Enough about them, what's going on with Patrick?"

"He's been on tenterhooks waiting for his plane to leave on Friday, he's so excited to meet his mother."

"What's the plan? Is he still going to surprise her, or is he calling to prepare her?"

"He wants to see her reaction in person. He's worried if he calls her, she'll tell him not to come. If things go well, he's going to stay there through the next weekend so they can get to know each other, and then, if they agree, we'll go back and spend Thanksgiving with her. The kids are excited to meet their new grandparent."

"November's a better month to be in Phoenix. It's so hot in the summer."

Patty stood. "Better get back. Patrick and I told the kids we'd take them out for burgers for lunch." She left.

"Mom, do I have clean socks?" Jenny called out the kitchen window.

"They're in the laundry basket."

Her face disappeared, and a moment later, she walked out the back door, swinging a tennis racket. "Going to volley with Jacob over at the park."

"Did you eat?"

She rolled her eyes and stomped out of the gate. "I'm not ten."

"Sometimes, I wonder." I sighed—one day at a time. The noon whistle blew, and no work was getting done with me sitting there, so I hoisted myself from the chair and walked into the house. I had grabbed a dust rag and started my routine when a knock sounded at the back door. Rob called, "Anyone home?"

"In here."

"Met the neighbors. They seem nice."

"They have a daughter a year younger than Jenny. Darn. I should have told Jenny to go over and ask if she plays tennis."

Rob hugged me. "There'll be time. They looked like they were pretty busy unloading. I offered to help, but they said they have a system. Can I twist your arm and take you to lunch?"

I held it out. "Twist away."

"I have an ulterior motive."

"Uh-oh."

"How would you feel about us going to the lake this weekend?"

"I don't know. It's been so busy." I picked up my purse.

"That's the point. We haven't had any downtime. Between my mother being suspected of killing her husband, her quick remarriage, and Jenny taking off for London, it's been crazy. Besides which, I'd love some alone time with you." He pulled me toward him.

"It has been stressful. Maybe we could." I smiled. "Let's do it. I'll ask Patty if Jenny can stay with them."

CHAPTER 6

Patrick

My mother. How odd to think of someone other than my adoptive mom that way. It's been forty-one years since she gave me up, and if she had tried, she could have found me. After all, she married my father after giving me up. Between the two of them, they should have searched for me. I shook two aspirin into my hand and popped them in my mouth, draining what was left of the water in my cup.

The flight attendant maneuvered the cart down the aisle, collecting trash. I handed her the empty. Just before five, Phoenix time. *Should I go to the hotel first? Or should I meet my mother?*

The flight attendant's voice came over the loudspeaker. "In preparation for landing, please make sure all carry-ons are stowed, your tray tables are in the upright and locked position, and your seatbelts are securely fastened."

Baggage claim in Phoenix is always such a mess. I'll have plenty of time to decide later. The plane landed, and I joined the throng jostling to get off. As per usual, the baggage claim carousel number changed three times while I waited. I grabbed my bag and walked out the door.

The heat took my breath away. It felt as if I were opening the door to hell. Why on earth was I in Phoenix in the summer? I hopped on the rental car bus and was eventually deposited by a generic car where I stowed my luggage, turned on the air conditioner, and stared at the navigation screen. *Hotel or Mother?* I typed in my mother's address. I'd survey the scene and then decide.

The house was a sprawling Spanish hacienda with manicured gardens, a red-tiled roof, and a great view of Squaw Peak. It had to be all of eight thousand square feet sitting on at least two acres of land. My mouth dropped. *She must have money.* My foot hit the brake, and I came to a stop just past the front walkway. My mouth felt like I had been traveling for days in the Sahara, so I took a quick sip of water and pushed open the door. *There's no time like the present to be rejected. Maybe I could get a red-eye and be back with the kids and Patty tomorrow.* I trudged to the beautiful arched front door, which was surrounded by flowering red bougainvillea. It was set in an alcove with some kind of pale marble tile and blue accents. *Patty would love this.* I took a deep breath, shut my eyes, and pressed the doorbell. A petite woman with carefully coiffed white hair and piercing blue eyes answered. My heart raced. She was shorter and chicer than I had imagined, and finally coming face-to-face with her, I felt like I'd been hit by a Mack truck. My jaw dropped.

"Yes?" Her eyes widened as she clutched her chest and staggered back. "Frank? No. It can't be. Frank's dead."

I reached out my hand to steady her. "My name is Patrick Twilliger. I'm your son."

She paled and gasped. "I need to sit down." She led me to a cozy sitting room on the left side of the front door.

"I'm so sorry. I didn't mean just to blurt it."

She collapsed onto one of the white facing sofas, fanning herself with one hand.

"Would you like water? I'm sure I'd be able to find—"

"Just give me a moment."

I focused on the ebony stained bookcases and watercolors decorating the walls and tried to slow the racing of my heart. I wiped the sweat from my hands onto my pants and tried to figure out what to say. I blurted, "Um. It's a beautiful room."

Color crept back into her face. "It's such a shock. You look just like your father did at your age." Her head tilted. "Of course, he had brown eyes. Yours are blue. Like mine."

"Are you sure you're okay?"

"It's an amazing resemblance. I'll be right back." She strode from the room and returned a moment later with a framed photo of a man in an army uniform. "See? Here's a picture of Frank before I met him. He was so young then."

I took it from her. *He really did look like me.* I touched his face. It was the other way around; I looked like him—*my father.*

"Where are my manners? Tea?"

"Iced tea, if you have any." I shook my head, trying to regain composure.

She stared at me as if she was in a trance. I shifted from foot to foot under her scrutiny. She jumped. "Woolgathering. Let's go to the kitchen." She led me past an enormous great room dominated by a molded Kiva fireplace. The kitchen was just as stunning, with Saltillo tile floors, gleaming white quartz countertops, and a rough-hewn wooden kitchen island.

"My wife would love your house. She's an interior designer."

She struggled with taking a full pitcher of iced tea from the refrigerator, put it on the counter, and filled two tall glasses with ice.

"Would you like me to pour?"

"Would you? It's a bit heavy for me. I keep telling Matilda to put it into a smaller container, but she likes the way this one looks."

I turned it in my hand. "It's a nice pitcher. Who's Matilda?"

"My cook. It's her day off."

"Oh." I poured the tea into the glasses and wandered to the black-framed French doors. They led to an outdoor patio, which surrounded a large pool. I pointed. "Do you swim?"

She chuckled. "Not as much as I used to. I do try to get out for laps at least three times a week. I'm not getting any younger, so I need to work at keeping in shape. Sugar?"

"Lemon, if you have it."

She took a bowl of cut lemons from the refrigerator. "Here you go."

I squeezed one into my drink and took a sip. "Perfect."

"I'm glad you like it. Shall we sit here?" She pointed to the stools lined up on one side of the island. "It's a bit hot to be outside."

"I nearly melted going between the airport and the rental car bus." I sat, and she joined me, hands worrying, and then suddenly she reached out and touched my face. I jerked back.

Her face looked stricken. "It's just such a shock. I can't believe you're here in my kitchen. I've dreamed of this so many times." She put her hand in her lap.

I touched it. "It's okay. You just took me by surprise.

She sat up and squared her shoulders. "There are probably some important questions I should ask, but most are so mundane, like— "What do you do? Do you have children? Where do you live? How did you find me?" She laughed. "I don't think I've ever asked so many questions in a string before." Her eyes welled.

"Let me see if I can remember them all. I sell cars for a living, Patty and I have four kids, and we live in a small town called Hopeful."

"Four grandchildren I didn't know I had." She stared out the window. After a moment, she continued, "Frank's son has three, but I've always thought of them as his. They have Frank's first wife as their grandmother on this side. We tried to make it work, especially when Frank was alive, but it's always been kind of awkward."

She sat back in the chair. "You didn't answer the last question. It was a closed adoption; how did you find me? I'm happy you did, but I'm puzzled."

"That's kind of a long story, and I'm getting hungry. The tiny bag of peanuts from the plane didn't hold me for long. May I take you out for dinner?"

"If you're up for it, there's a Mexican place not too far. I hope you don't mind driving, I prefer to leave that to others when I can."

The front door opened, and a woman called, "Helen, are you here?"

A trim, good-looking blonde in her late twenties, wearing shorts and a t-shirt, strode into the kitchen. "I saw great avocados at the market, and they had your name written all over—" she stopped. "I'm sorry, I didn't realize you had company."

I stood and held out my hand. "Patrick Twilliger."

She shook it.

"Katie, this will surprise you, but Patrick is my son. I opened the door, and there he stood after forty-one years." Tears rolled down her cheeks. "I never thought I'd see the day. I thought he was gone forever."

"I didn't realize you had a son."

Helen pulled a tissue from her pocket and dabbed her eyes.

"Can't wait to hear this story." Katie took a bowl from the cupboard and deposited the avocados into it.

Helen grabbed my hand. "It is quite a story, but it will have to wait. We're leaving for an early dinner."

"How fun. I'll get out of your hair." As she passed me, her eyes narrowed, "Take good care of Helen. She's one of my favorites."

I escorted Helen to the car and opened the door for her. "What should I call you?"

"Why don't we start with Helen, for now?"

"Helen it is. Where to?" She gave me turn-by-turn directions, and after a few minutes, we pulled into the parking lot of La Hacienda Deliciosa. It dominated a small storefront and was decorated in the colors of the Mexican flag. I parked and helped Helen from the car.

She said, "It may not look like much, but the food is wonderful."

The hostess held the door. The restaurant was crowded, but there was an empty small Formica table for two near the window. I held Helen's seat, and she smiled. "Such a gentleman. You must have been brought up well."

The waiter put down tortilla chips, dip, and two large glasses of water. I took a chip, scooped the pico de gallo, and deposited it into my mouth. It tasted great. Then came the fire. I gasped and choked, and my eyes watered. I grabbed for my glass and drained it. The waiter filled it again, and I drank half. When I could speak, I asked, "What's in that?"

"Just a smattering of ghost peppers." She took a chip, dipped it, and ate, without missing a beat.

I wiped my eyes with the napkin. "How can you stand it?"

"I love spicy food. Always have. Frank couldn't abide it." She waved the waiter over. "Would you please bring us the mild pico?"

He complied.

I picked up another chip, hesitated, then took the plunge. I tensed, waiting for the burn. There was just a slight bit of heat. "This is more my speed."

Helen ordered her "usual," a chicken mole, and I ordered a shrimp dish Helen thought was safe for me. After the waiter left, she touched my hand. "How did you find me?"

"My wife ordered a DNA testing kit for my birthday. I swabbed the insides of my cheeks and sent it away for analysis. Do you know how that works?"

"Vaguely. I've seen commercials for it."

"The results are pretty general. They tell you where your ancestors came from. My results showed Northern Europe. And, the biggest percentages were from Ireland-England, and the next highest was from Germany-France."

Helen's head tilted. "That sounds right."

"Next, I opted in for any relatives to contact me. James reached out."

She sat back in her chair. "He told you where to find me."

I nodded.

"But I talked to him two nights ago, and he didn't mention anything."

"I told him I wanted to tell you myself."

She put her hand on my arm. "I'm glad."

Our dinners arrived. My shrimp were perfectly cooked with just a tiny kick. After the dinner plates were cleared, and I had ordered a flan, Helen cleared her throat. "I guess you want to know what happened. Why I gave you up."

"I've always wondered, but I don't want to rush you. If you're not comfortable—"

"It was the toughest decision of my life." She coughed and took a sip of water. "I was older and had given up on finding love, but then I met your father. We worked at the same company. I was in accounting, and he was someone who was going to the top. I thought he was so handsome, and we fell in love. After a few months, he fessed up—he told me he was married, so I broke it off. And, then—" she paused. "—I found out I was pregnant.

"Times were different in those days. Today, it seems people think nothing of having children out of wedlock. But back then, it just wasn't done. If Frank hadn't already been married, he would have married me, and life would have been so different—" Helen's voice trailed off, and she seemed frozen, staring at a spot behind me.

After a moment, I said, "Helen? Are you all right? We could do this another time."

She shuddered as if coming out of a trance. "Where was I? Frank helped with the bills, of course, I didn't ask him to, but he wanted to. When I was eight months pregnant, I saw his wife come out of a store. I scrunched down, and she didn't see me. She was pregnant. Not as big as me, but as I later found out, about four months behind me. Frank was never going to leave her. Not now that she was pregnant.

"Right then and there, I made the toughest decision of my life. I decided to give the baby up for adoption." Her hand flew to her mouth. "I decided to give *you* up for adoption."

She twisted her napkin. "It was hard, but I was thirty, had to work to support myself, and was all alone. It was too much. The stigma—it was as if I had been permanently branded with the letter 'A.' I had to find a new job—afterward. I needed a fresh start from all the whispering behind my back—everyone speculating about the identity of the father." Tears slid down her face.

"Then, seven years later, I opened the door, and Frank stood on my stoop. He had decided to leave his family. He told me I was his one true love, and his only shot at being happy. I took him back, and two years later, we were married."

I rubbed my neck. "Why didn't you try to find me after that?"

Her eyes teared. "It was a closed adoption. I didn't know how to find you, and you had been with your new family for nine years. Even if I could have found you, I couldn't do that to you or your adoptive parents. So, I tried to be happy with the little time we got with Frank's son, and his children now, of course. James still visits me, you know."

"He told me." I paid the bill. "Thanks for being honest with me."

She grabbed my hand. "You have to believe that giving you up was an agonizing decision."

I stood, my stomach churning. "It's a lot to take in. Let's get you home."

I pulled up in front of her house and escorted her to the door. She stood on her toes and kissed my cheek. "I'm glad you're here. Where are you staying?"

"The Phoenician. My boss has a connection, so they gave me a deal."

She said, "That's nice—if you want to save even more money, you could think about staying here."

"Let's take our time and get to know each other." I patted her arm.

* * *

I called Patty when I returned to the hotel room.

She sounded panicked when she picked up the phone. "What? What happened?"

"I just wanted to tell you about dinner with my mother."

"Do you know what time it is?"

I checked my watch. "Sorry. I didn't realize it was so late."

"I waited and gave up at midnight. Just got to sleep." She yawned.

"Sorry."

There was a pause, then dull thuds. She came back on the line. "Okay. My pillows are fluffed, and I've propped myself up in bed. I'm ready to talk. How did it go?"

"You're tired. We can talk tomorrow."

"Oh no, you don't. I'm awake now. Tell me."

I did. At the end of the story, Patty asked, "How did you feel when she told you they decided not to try and find you?"

"It was a kick in the gut. But, I feel sorry for her. It had to have been hard to be in that situation. Having children, I couldn't imagine giving any of them up. No matter what the circumstance."

"You're a good father, and the children and I love you. What's next?"

"Lunch with her tomorrow."

"Call me afterward."

* * *

By six the next morning, I was out for a run. I woke early because of the time change and decided the day wasn't going to get any cooler as it progressed. The sweat on my face evaporated almost immediately, which gave me a slight chill. I rounded the corner for the hotel and was glad a cup of coffee was in sight.

Helen's friend, Katie, was sitting in the lobby. I filled a mug and joined her. "This is a surprise. Are you visiting someone?"

"You."

My eyes widened. "How did you know where I was staying?"

"Helen called me last night to talk after your dinner. She mentioned it. Why don't you take a seat?"

I looked down at my shorts and t-shirt. "Can it wait a few minutes? I'd like to take a quick shower."

"Sure. I'll be here." She picked up one of the lobby newspapers and sat.

I ran up the stairs to my room and hopped in the shower. *What on earth does she want?* A quick shave later, I dressed and made my way to the lobby. I sat in a chair facing Katie. "I guess you and Helen are good friends."

"The best."

"How did you meet? There's quite an age difference."

"The theater."

"That's nice."

"Helen didn't have any family in town, so I became her family. Then you appeared out of the blue. How do we know you're who you say you are? You could be anyone. She's delighted you found her, but this could be a scam." She frowned.

"Didn't she talk to James?"

"Even if she did, you could be scamming him too."

I stood. "Thank you for your concern, but this is a private matter. If my mother wants me to prove who I am, I'll do it."

Her face reddened, and she got to her feet. "I'll talk to Helen. You better bring your proof to lunch today." She stalked out the door.

I sank back onto the chair, used my phone to log into the DNA site, and downloaded a copy of the report showing I was a sibling match to James. In a way, I understood Katie's concern and was happy Helen had a friend to look out for her. But it made me mad all the same. I couldn't help it. I was given up at birth, and now I had to prove who I was?

I had just sat down to breakfast when James turned the corner into the hotel's cafe.

He sat next to me. "What, no hug for your long-lost brother?"

My mouth dropped, and I did an awkward one-armed embrace. "What are you doing in Phoenix? I thought you were coming to visit Helen in November."

"Business; we're having trouble with a client, and since I knew you'd be here, I volunteered."

"Have you had breakfast?"

"Not yet." He ordered and then turned to me. "I surprised Helen when I arrived late last night. I always stay with her when I'm in town."

"That's nice." I sipped my coffee. Our meals came.

"I don't want to horn in on your reunion, but I was hoping we could all have dinner. It'll be Helen and her two boys."

I shifted in my seat. "We hadn't planned that far ahead, but if she's up for it—"

James leaned back, hand to heart. "If you'd rather be alone, I understand. It's just this trip came up—"

"Don't be silly, it's fine. I'll see you later. I want to give Patty a quick call now the kids have left for camp."

I strolled to the stairs, took them two at a time back to my room, and pressed speed dial for my wife.

"Hi, honey. What's up?" She answered the phone.

"You wouldn't believe the morning I'm having."

"Try me."

"Guess who was waiting for me when I got back from my run this morning?"

"Helen?"

"Her apparent best friend who is way younger than me."

"So?"

I sat at the desk. "She wants proof I am me."

"That's nice she's looking out for Helen."

"Whatever. Then James showed up at breakfast."

"James, your brother? Did you know he was going to be in town?"

"It was a surprise. He's staying with Helen," I groused.

"You don't sound happy."

"He said we'd go out to dinner tonight. 'Helen and her two boys.' She only has one son, me. But he was able to grow up with her, to know her. I'm starting from ground zero."

"Honey, it's going to take you a while to work through all of this, don't push it. And, try to be nice to everyone."

I sighed. "I'll try. I have to meet Helen in two hours. I'm going to kill time at the Heard Museum. They have a good Anasazi collection."

"Try to relax. I'll talk to you later. Love you."

"Love you too. Kiss the kids for me." I hung up.

Helen said, "I'm so embarrassed. I can't believe Katie went to your hotel. Of course, you're my son; you look just like Frank. Who else could you be?"

I handed her my phone and enlarged the document from the DNA company. "See here—it says James is a sibling match to me."

She glanced at it and then set my phone down. "We don't need to talk about this again; you're my son."

I smiled. "This restaurant is beautiful." The outdoor terrace had high arches, and purple blooming sage dominated the landscape. The eighteenth green was a hundred yards away, and golfers were intent on their putts.

"It is. And, the misters make it bearable." Helen's salad and my salmon burger arrived. Her hand snaked over for one of my fries. "I hope you don't mind, but no one I know gets them anymore. I shouldn't but—"

I inched my plate closer to her. "Enjoy. I shouldn't eat them either, but I'm going to."

She grinned and snagged another. "Speaking of James, he surprised me last night. He had an unexpected business trip. I hope you don't mind, but I asked him to dinner tonight."

"I ran into him this morning at breakfast. That's fine."

* * *

I met Helen and James at the entrance of the restaurant. It seemed far more upscale than anything I'd seen so far. Crisp white linens, gold chargers, and flowering miniature cacti adorned the tables. James led the way. "This place is my favorite."

"I know how much you like spicy food." Helen caressed James's cheek. "Patrick is not a fan, but there are several dishes I think he can handle."

James laughed. "A wimp like Dad."

"Those ghost peppers from last night still haunt me." I put my napkin in my lap.

"Pun intended?" Helen asked.

"Yes." I smiled.

James patted Helen's hand. "I'm glad I got the chance to come to town. I've missed you."

"I love seeing you. And, it's even more special now Patrick is here. My two boys." She cleared her throat and turned toward me. "I couldn't sleep last night after meeting you. All my life I've dreamed you'd find me, and now you have." She patted my hand and cleared her throat. "I'm not getting any younger, so I've scheduled a meeting with my attorney. Now that we've reunited, it's time for me to take another look at my will."

"But most of that money was Dad's." James's face reddened.

"James, Patrick is Frank's son too. And, he is my only child. I'm meeting with my attorney."

"If you'll excuse me, I'm not feeling well." James stood, threw his napkin on his chair, and stalked away.

I started to rise, and Helen stopped me. "He'll get over it. He has a bad temper, but once he's had a chance to think, he'll realize I'm right."

"I hope you understand I didn't reach out to you for money. I came because I wanted to meet you. To find out if we could have a relationship."

"We can. But I'm old enough to know not to put things off. I'm still going to meet with my attorney. Enough on that subject. Tell me more about my beautiful grandchildren."

* * *

After I dropped Helen off, I went back to the hotel. I couldn't get comfortable and started to pace from the bathroom to the window and back again. *How different my life would have been if I had lived here.* On my fifth turn, I scooped up the keys from the dresser and walked out the door. I drove aimlessly and suddenly realized I was only a few blocks from Helen's. I course-corrected and slid to a stop in front of her house.

James was home; his car was in the driveway as I turned the corner. What would he think if I waltzed up to the front door and announced I was moving my things from the hotel? Helen had invited me. Since he had been upset earlier about the money, I don't think he'd greet me with open arms.

I frowned as I stared holes in the house. It should be me staying with my mother, not him. My face heated up, and I felt like the kid who got picked last at baseball. They didn't want me. Not my father, my mother, or my brother. They all had fine lives without me.

My phone buzzed, and I pulled it from my pocket. An automated bank alert—my mortgage payment had gone out. I clicked to dismiss it, and the background photo appeared. It was my favorite picture of me with my family. We were at Merry's lake house, and she had captured all of us balancing on a large unicorn float she used to have. We looked relaxed, tan, and incredibly happy. That was such a fun day. And it was one of too many to count. I may have missed out on a life in Phoenix, but I wouldn't trade my life for anything. I smiled and pulled away from the curb.

CHAPTER 7

Merry

By Friday morning, I was packed and ready for the trip to the lake. I ran down the stairs into the kitchen, opened the wine fridge, and retrieved a bottle of champagne. It was time to celebrate surviving the last few months. I texted my assistant, Cheryl, to make sure everything was going smoothly at my business, The Meredith March Insurance Agency. She gave the all-clear, so I poked my head out the front door. Rob was just pulling into the drive. I called up the stairs, "I'm leaving. Text if you need anything."

Jenny came out of her room and sat on the top step. "You're only gone for the weekend. I'll be fine."

"I don't want to leave you alone, and Patty's expecting you at her house in an hour. Don't be late."

She rolled her eyes as only a teenager can do. "Mom, I'm not a kid."

"Like you haven't made bad choices." I swung the suitcase out the door and followed it.

Rob grabbed the bag and champagne. He laughed and pointed to the bottle already in his car. "Great minds think alike."

"Two champagnes are better than one." I grinned as I slid onto the passenger seat. "I've put together some ideas of things we can do. There's a garlic festival on Saturday, and an art show on Sunday."

"Or, we could just chill." He started the car.

"That too." I reclined the seat, turned the radio to nineties tunes, and hummed along. After an hour, we left the highway, and tall evergreens lined the two-lane road. I rolled down the window to breathe air tinted with the smell of pine, and my shoulders relaxed. Shortly afterward, we pulled into the drive.

I jumped out of the car and stretched. "Oh, good. The landscaping crew came. The raft is in the water, and the lounge chairs are on the dock. Everything looks so inviting."

"I thought we might not want to go out, so I brought provisions." Rob pulled a cooler from the trunk.

I kissed him on the nose. "What a good idea."

"Finally alone. I've missed you." He pulled me closer for a deep kiss.

A car drove by, and someone shouted, "Get a room."

"What a terrific idea." I grabbed my suitcase and walked into the cabin.

✳ ✳ ✳

The weekend was just what I needed. We swam, played board games, and slept in. On Sunday morning, I lazed in bed, watching the early morning light play off the water. Rob handed me a cup of coffee and said, "I can't believe we have to leave today. We should have made it a longer weekend."

I kissed his cheek. "I love being able to spend so much time with you. And, beating you at backgammon was fun too."

He tapped my head with a pillow. "I felt bad for you after you lost three games of Yahtzee."

I groaned. "Don't remind me. What do you want to do today?"

"I thought you'd never ask." He slid into bed.

An hour later, I hopped into the shower, and Rob left for the bait shop, which did double duty on Sundays as a bagel place. Drying my hair, I couldn't help but smile. Life was good. I donned pink shorts and a white polo shirt and traipsed down the stairs. The Sunday paper was on the table. I retrieved it, poured fresh coffee, and made my way down the flagstone path to the chairs overlooking the lake. The sky was a deep blue dotted at the far horizon with white puffy clouds. I pulled out the comic section and began to read.

Rob shouted, "Need more coffee?"

I waved. "I'm good."

He walked down the path, carrying a tray.

"Yum. Bagels. Thanks for getting them."

"I looked for lox, but they didn't have any."

"Not surprising. It's odd enough they carry night crawlers and bagels." I spread a sesame seed one with cream cheese. "These are so good."

"They have quite the setup. They parboil the bagels in water and then bake them."

"That's what makes them so chewy." My phone rang. "Hi, Patty. What's up?"

"It's Patrick's mom. She's dead."

I gasped and sat back in the chair. "His adoptive mother? Or his birth mother."

"The one in Phoenix—birth mother."

"That's terrible. He just met her. They spent all that time apart, and now she's dead? What happened?" I rubbed the back of my neck.

"He doesn't know. He and his half-brother took her to dinner at a Mexican place last night. She picked the place; apparently, she loves spicy food and margaritas. Loved spicy food. I can't believe it. He was so upset when he called."

"I'm sorry. What can I do?"

"I have a flight tonight at six. I hate to ask, but do you think you could stay at my house with the kids until we figure out a plan?"

"Of course."

Rob touched my shoulder. "Does she need a ride to the airport?

Before I had a chance to ask, Patty said, "Ed's picking me up at four, so I have that covered. Andy's on a buying trip, so he was free." Ed and Andy lived behind me and ran a combo antique shop and café called Tempting Treasures and Tasty Treats.

"We'll be home before you leave. Please let Patrick know how sorry we are." I hung up and turned to Rob. "We should get going." I stood, gathered the newspaper, and lifted the tray.

"I'll take that." Rob deposited his mug on the tray and took it from me. "How terrible for Patrick. To be reunited for so brief a time."

"At least they were able to meet before she died." We walked into the house. "I'll grab the sheets and pack the things we have upstairs. Could you put the trash in the bin by the road and put whatever needs to come with us in the cooler?"

Rob pulled me close. "Your wish is my command."

I swatted him on the butt. "Let's get moving."

Forty-five minutes later, we headed toward home. I played with the radio, and we listened to jazz. As Rob made the turn from the highway, I said, "Thanks for suggesting this weekend. It was nice to have a break, even if we had to cut it a bit short."

He pulled into my driveway. "Dinner tonight?"

"If you don't mind eating with five kids."

"As long as you're there, it'll be perfect."

I kissed him and got out of the car. "Bring pizza."

"Will do." He backed out.

I hurried in the door, dumped the clothes from the lake in the laundry room, and packed what I'd need for the next few days. Next, I made sure the cats had fresh water and food. They were vocal in their disapproval of my absence. "Don't worry. I'll be back tomorrow to see you." I hopped in the car and drove to Patty's.

Ed was loading her suitcase in his car, and Patty looked harried. I hugged her. "Are you okay?"

"It's sad I didn't get to meet her. But at least Patrick did. I called my mom. She and my dad will be here tomorrow to relieve you."

"I could have stayed longer."

"They love being with the kids. I'll call when I know more."

Ed looked at his watch. "Need to get a move on." Patty got in his car, and they left.

I pushed the back door open. Patty's daughter, Cindy, and my daughter, Jenny, were in the kitchen, making cookies. I hugged Cindy. "I'm sorry about your grandmother."

She returned the hug and then continued placing cookie dough on the sheet. "It's weird. We never met her. I'm not sure how I feel."

I rubbed her arm. "I'm sure you would have liked her."

Jenny popped the cookies into the oven and set the timer. "I'm sorry you never met her. I'm sure she was a nice person."

Patty's three other kids raced into the kitchen. Her youngest ran to me. "When's Mommy coming home?"

His brother hit his arm. "She told us she'd call later. Ms. March doesn't know, stupid."

I grabbed Shawn's arm. "No hitting. And, don't call your brother stupid."

He looked somewhat ashamed. "Sorry. When are the cookies going to be ready?"

Jenny said, "A few more minutes."

"Rob's bringing pizza for dinner, so don't eat too many cookies."

"With pepperoni?"

"Of course."

Shawn said, "Call us when the cookies are done." The three ran from the kitchen like birds flocking in formation.

* * *

Two hours later, Rob walked through the door, balancing three pies. "Who's hungry?" He was swarmed. "Let me put them down first."

I pointed to the island. "Put them there. I've already set the table."

Dinner was a raucous affair, and we had the remaining cookies for dessert. Finally, the smaller kids were in bed, and Cindy and Jenny had gone up to play a video game.

I collapsed next to Rob on the sofa. "Every time I think it might be nice to have another child, I come here. They're exhausting."

He put his arm around me. "You're so good with them, so patient. Does this mean you don't want any more kids?"

"Jenny will be out of the house next fall, and I'll be forty in a few months. I'm not sure I could do this again."

"But we'd have such cute kids."

"This sounds like a serious discussion we need to have, and right now, I'm exhausted."

He kissed my cheek. "Another glass of wine?"

"That I can do."

CHAPTER 8

Patrick

It was a depressing ride to the airport. I couldn't believe it had only been a few days since I arrived; everything looked so brown and dingy. I parked and strode to baggage claim. After only a few minutes, I spied Patty and waved.

She ran to me and gave me a big hug. "I'm so sorry about your mother."

"It's unbelievable. We enjoyed a nice dinner, I dropped her at the house, and went back to the hotel. I should have gone in the house with her, instead of just dropping her off. She wanted me to come in, but after James stormed away at dinner, I thought it would be better if she had time alone with him." He sighed.

"Did she have any kind of discomfort at dinner?"

"She was fine."

"Hopefully, she didn't suffer."

I pulled up in front of the house and parked.

Patty whistled. "That's some huge hacienda."

"Wait till you see the inside. With your interior decorator eye, you'll appreciate it even more." I opened the car door for Patty, and we walked to the entry.

As we approached, James came out of the house and hugged Patty. "I'm happy to see you again, even in these sad circumstances."

"I'm so sorry for your loss," she said.

I shook James's hand. "Thanks for calling to let me know. I'm sorry about last night."

"My fault entirely. Doesn't matter much now anyway." James extended his arm toward the house. "We're in the living room. Katie's here, and she's pretty shook-up, as you can imagine."

Katie was seated on the sofa. Her eyes were red and swollen, and she clutched a tissue in one hand. I introduced her to Patty. "This is Helen's good friend, Katie."

Patty shook her hand. "I'm so sorry."

I sat on the love seat facing the sofa, and Patty sat next to me. James said, "We're having a mimosa, Helen's favorite drink. Would you care to join us?"

Patty shook her head. "Maybe water. I'm dehydrated from the plane."

"Ice?" James took a bottle of water from the small fridge in the bar.

"Please."

"What about you, bro?"

"I'll have a mimosa."

James handed us our drinks.

Patty took a long swig. "Have you heard anything more from the police?"

"It was probably a heart attack." James sat next to Katie.

Katie dabbed her eyes. "Probably the shock from the recent surprise in her life."

"Me?" My face heated up.

Patty pulled my hand onto her lap. "Had she been ill? Did she have heart problems?"

"She was in good health. That's what makes it so odd." Katie nodded toward me. "She was with you at dinner last night, right?"

"She was with Patrick and me." James leaned forward. "Why?"

"Was she upset; was there some type of fight?" Tears ran down her face. "There just has to be a reason."

"I was kind of a jerk, but I apologized afterward." James's face paled. "You don't think that had anything to do with this, do you?"

I shook my head. "She didn't seem upset when I dropped her off."

Katie pointed at me. "Then it must have been you. Why did you have to show up?"

I stood. "I had nothing to do with this."

Patty got to her feet. "I'm more tired than I thought after the trip. Take me back to the hotel."

"Please don't leave." James turned to Katie. "I know you're upset, but you can't blame Patrick. This wasn't his fault."

"Patty's tired from the flight. We'll see you tomorrow." I turned and walked out the door. Patty hurried to keep up with my long strides. After I slid into the car, I turned to her. "What if Katie's right? What if the shock of seeing me killed Helen? How will I live with that?"

* * *

I woke at eight the next morning. Patty was reading in the chair and looked like she'd been up for hours.

I kissed her on my way to the shower. "I didn't sleep well last night, and I won't be able to get a run in this morning. There's a coffee shop downstairs—can you grab breakfast while I get ready?"

I put the shower on the hardest spray and let it play on my back. *We should go to the Desert Botanical Garden today.* Walking around the garden would be a welcome respite from thinking about Helen. Katie stumped me, though. How could she believe the shock of seeing me caused my mother's death? My shoulders tensed as I rinsed. I turned off the spray, toweled dry, and put on shorts. Coffee perfumed the air. Good, Patty was back.

She was hunched over the desk, eating a plain donut. "I got you a raspberry-filled one with powdered sugar."

I retrieved another towel from the bathroom and draped it over my shorts as I sat, to stop the sugar from getting everywhere.

Patty finished eating the donut and sipped her coffee. "How are you feeling today?"

"Better." I carefully lifted the towel and shook it over the bathroom sink. "Ready to go?"

* * *

I pulled into the entrance of the Desert Botanical Garden and found one of the last parking spots. I handed Patty a bottle of sunscreen. "Unless you want to look like a boiled lobster, you may want to put this on. The sun is stronger than you think."

After slathering lotion on her face and arms, she retrieved a hat and sunglasses from a bag.

I opened the door. "Ready?"

She gasped. "It's almost hard to breathe. Are you sure you want to do this?"

"We may as well see the sights. It's not like we'll be coming back to visit. Besides, look at the clouds on the horizon, maybe we'll get lucky with some shade."

We paid admission, bought two bottles of water, and then set out on the Wildflower Loop Trail. I didn't think I was going that fast, but Patty pulled on my arm and said, "Can we adopt a more meandering speed?"

"Sorry. I'm still wound up. I can't believe Helen's gone."

"Try to relax for a while. Look at the pretty blooms. I didn't think much flowered in the desert. I love all the sage and cacti." She rubbed my back.

I slowed my pace. Succulents surrounded us in various shades of green, blooming in vibrant shades of orange, magenta, and yellow.

Thunder clapped, and Patty's face jerked skyward. "I didn't think it stormed in Phoenix."

One of the guides hurried toward us. "Unless you want to get drenched, you may want to hoof it to the restaurant. It's monsoon season." She ran to another group.

Patty's eyebrow arched. "Monsoons? Don't they only happen in Asia?"

"Let's have this discussion inside." I took Patty's arm as the wind began to blow, and we hurried to the restaurant. "Are you hungry? We could do an early lunch."

"Starving. That donut didn't fill me up."

We walked into Gertrude's just as the skies opened, and torrential rains began.

Patty's mouth gaped. "Thank heavens the guide told us to take cover."

"We would have been drenched."

The waiter handed us menus. I pointed. "I know what you're getting."

"You think you know me so well." She surveyed the menu.

The waiter returned. Patty said, "I'll have the duck, medium rare, please."

I laughed. "I knew it. I'll have the Gertie Burger, medium well, with crispy bacon."

"A hamburger?"

"I need something comforting."

Patty held my hand. "I'm sorry Katie made you feel bad."

"I just wish that my last conversation with Helen hadn't been about money."

"I've been wondering—you don't think James killed her, do you? Because she was thinking about changing her will."

"You and Merry have been investigating too many murders lately. Helen died in bed. She wasn't murdered."

"Are you sure?"

"Yes. And, I've made a decision."

"What's that?"

"I want to bury Helen at home."

Patty's eyebrow lifted. "In Hopeful?"

"In the church graveyard. That way, we can visit her."

CHAPTER 9

Merry

Somehow I had gotten the three youngest out of the house in time for band camp. Feeling accomplished, I treated myself to a donut and coffee. Mid-bite, Patty called from Phoenix. I quipped, "Isn't it early there?"

"I'm still on our time. I almost fell asleep on my dinner plate last night. I don't know what it is about western time zones, but it seems like one minute you're full of energy, and the next, you hit a wall. Patrick's still sleeping, so I snuck out by the pool."

"How's it going?"

"It's been a little crazy. Helen had a close friend named Katie, who thinks the surprise of meeting Patrick killed Helen."

"But from what you told me, she was ecstatic that he came."

"So we thought, but maybe Katie's right. I wouldn't say this to Patrick, but Helen was older; maybe the shock was too much for her. It's too depressing to think about." Paper crackled.

"What are you eating?"

"Yodels."

"For breakfast?" I dunked the donut in coffee and took a bite.

"Don't judge. I was hungry, and there wasn't much of a selection in the vending machine by the pool."

I eyed the rest of my calorie-laden repast. "When do you think you'll get back?"

"Hopefully, early next week. We're meeting James at the funeral home today." There was a splash. "Just had to put my toes in the water. It feels so good. My parents should get there around three. Could you make sure the kids get home from band camp okay? That way, if they're late, I don't have to worry."

"No problem. Call me with an update when you get a chance." I hung up and put the mug and plate in the dishwasher. A quick swipe of the counter and I strolled out the door to the office.

Although it wasn't warm, the high humidity made the walk less pleasant. Some people were out early, mowing their lawns. I waved to a client and mouthed, "Smart idea." He nodded and continued making straight even rows on his textbook green grass. *Hate to see his water bill.*

Cheryl greeted me at the door, pad and pen in hand. "Getting hot out there."

"Better than snow."

"True." She led the way to my office. "I had to move your meetings around. Your last one is at two. Andy called. He wanted to have lunch with you later this week. Thursday looks good. Should I let him know?"

Cheryl's pen tapped her pad. Her gleaming blond hair had been brushed back into an elegant chignon. She wore a black pencil skirt with a matching jacket and looked every inch the professional she was. I tossed my purse into a desk drawer. "What would I do without you?"

"Like I'm going to allow you to find out?"

"Yes, to lunch with Andy. And, thanks for rearranging things for me today."

"Door open or shut?"

"Shut, please. I want to work on my call list." She closed the door, and I picked up the sheet of prospects and lifted the phone.

Two hours later, I stood, stretched, and opened the door. Cheryl looked up. "Everything okay?"

"Please bring in the file on the Customer Appreciation event next month."

She pulled a folder from a drawer, walked into the office, and sat. "What would you like to know?"

"Could you go over anything that's still outstanding? I want to make sure everything goes without a hitch."

"We were able to secure the shelter at the park, so that's done. The invitations have started to come back; we're at sixty 'Yeses' to five 'Noes.'" Her hand moved down the page. "The only things still to be done are the inventory of games, menu selection, and of course, your divine chocolate cupcakes."

"When do we have to finalize the menu?"

She pulled out a contract. "End of next week. I've scheduled time for us on Friday to talk about it. Here are a couple of sample menus they sent for you to take a look at."

"Anything strike your fancy?"

"The macaroni and cheese sticks look like fun."

My eyebrow rose.

"Think cake pops but with deep-fried balls of macaroni and cheese."

I coughed and hit my chest. "My arteries are clogging just thinking about them, but I'm sure they'll be a big hit with the kids."

She laughed. "And, the adults. Who are we kidding? I'll leave the menus with you. I've put stars by the ones I think you should consider." She walked out the door.

I scanned them. The standard hamburgers and hot dogs were listed, but also some different choices. *Satay chicken. Yum.* My mouth started to water. I pulled a yogurt from my refrigerator. *Not quite as good.*

* * *

After my two o'clock, I hurried out the door. The air felt saturated. There was a storm coming, but hopefully, the rain would cool the temperature. I turned onto Patty's driveway, where a massive dark blue SUV was parked near the door, hatch up. Patty's dad, Ned, maneuvered down the back steps and swung a suitcase from the back. He was north of seventy, with graying hair, and sparkling blue eyes. He put the bag down and extended his hand. "Merry, nice to see you again."

Jane, Patty's mom, poked her head out the door. "Is that Merry? Come in, dear, come in."

I grabbed her makeup case and handed it to her.

She smiled. "You didn't have to do that. Ned's perfectly capable of unpacking."

"Many hands make light work."

"Would you like tea?" Without waiting for an answer, she filled the kettle. Her previously brown tresses were now snow-white, but her face was remarkably unlined. Patty had good genes in her favor.

Ned walked in with a round tin. "Last thing."

"Is that what I hope it is?" I tapped the top of the container.

"I had just enough time to make Irish Soda bread last night before I went to bed." Jane kissed Ned on the cheek. "The kids would have been disappointed if they didn't have some when they got home."

I took out butter to soften. "They're going to want this too."

"Here you go." Jane put a mug in front of me.

Footsteps sounded from the front door. "Grandma, Grandpa!" The three youngest rounded the corner and crowded into the kitchen. "Did you make your bread?"

Jane laughed. "Of course."

CHAPTER 10

Patrick

The funeral home was appropriately somber with dark paneling and hushed lighting. Katie and James were already there when Patty and I walked in. James stood. "Glad you're here. Do you want to see what Katie and I were thinking about in terms of a casket?"

"I thought we were meeting at one by ourselves." I made a point of looking at Katie.

"I asked Katie to come because she knows all of Helen's friends. Face it, we're pretty lost in that regard. At any rate, Katie and I were just moping around the house, so we decided to come early."

Patty touched my arm. "That's fine. Lead the way."

They took us to a room full of caskets where Patty wandered the room, examining them. She gasped, and I walked to her side. She pointed at the price tag, which read twenty-five thousand dollars. Katie and James stood next to one a row over. It was handsome cherrywood with pale rose satin lining.

James said, "We think she would have liked this one."

"Did Helen want to be cremated?" Patty asked.

"Of course." Katie rubbed the sleek wood.

I frowned. "Wouldn't it be more prudent to pick a cheaper one? It seems a shame to select something so beautiful just to burn it."

James asked, "What would people think?"

"That we had common sense." I strode across the room to the plain pine boxes. "Something like this would be more appropriate."

Katie shook her head. "Helen was an important benefactor in this town. If we opt for anything less than this, it will reflect badly on her, and us. James and I spoke this morning, and we decided to have a memorial for her on Saturday, with the funeral on Sunday, putting her to rest next to Frank in Scottsdale."

My mouth dropped. "How could you decide something like that without talking to me?"

"You didn't even know Helen. I knew her for six years, and Patrick was her stepson. We know what she would have wanted."

"I'm her biological son. I may not have known her as well as you, but her blood runs through my veins."

James rounded the casket and embraced me. "Sorry, bro. Everyone's tense. Why don't we wait on this until after the meeting with Helen's attorney?"

Patty elbowed me, "Why didn't you tell me about the meeting."

"Didn't know." I shrugged.

"The attorney didn't contact you?" James's brow furrowed.

"No."

"Strange. Probably an oversight. The meeting's at three at Helen's house. You should be there."

I grunted. "I'll be there. Thanks for letting me know."

* * *

The lawyer had set up shop in Helen's office. His large size was at odds with the gold-trimmed white French desk that dominated the room. I was concerned his girth was too much for the delicate chair in which he sat. He stood and extended his hand as Patty, and I entered. "Good afternoon. I'm Scott Clarke, Helen's lawyer. You are Helen's biological child?"

I nodded.

"Can you provide proof of this assertion?"

I handed him the documents I printed from the DNA site.

James laughed and handed him the photo Helen had remarked on when I first arrived in Phoenix. "Look at him and look at this photo of my dad. Is there any doubt?"

"I assume you have some type of government identification?" Scott held out his hand, and I gave him my driver's license. He examined it. "For now, I will accept this, but I will likely need additional documentation from you as we proceed."

I tilted my head. "I don't understand. Helen said she was going to update her will, but that was at dinner the night she died. I'm sure she must not have had enough time."

"Helen emailed me about her intentions that evening. She was not a woman who dilly-dallied." He frowned. "But you are quite correct; I was not able to put the documents together before she died. We'll be working from her last will and testament, dated four years ago."

"I'm still confused. Why do you need me to gather additional documentation if she wasn't able to change her will?"

"Because you are named in her current will."

"But she didn't know who I was."

"Her will specified a bequest to any natural issue of hers." He pointed to me with his half-glasses. "That would be you. Now, if there are no other questions, I'll begin."

He read from the will. As he got to the part concerning bequests, James and Katie sat forward in their chairs. "To my dear friend Katie Glass, I hereby bequeath the sum of one hundred thousand dollars. To any issue from my body, still living, otherwise to his issue, I hereby bequeath this house, a household account of one million dollars from which to pay for its upkeep and the household staff, and the additional sum of one million dollars. The remainder of my estate I bequeath to my stepson, James."

"A million dollars? And this house?" Patty gasped.

I put my arm around her. "Later."

63

"Those are the material bequests. There is one other stipulation. If you or you—" Scott pulled his glasses down on his nose and pointed to James and me in turn. "—were to die within the next twelve days, the money that person would have received goes to the remaining heir. There are also some minor gifts to the staff and charitable donations, but we can talk about those later."

He pulled out another paper. "Now, as to her final instructions for her funeral." He read through a lot of legalize, then said, "She wanted to be cremated. As to the rest, she leaves the ceremony and her final resting place up to her natural issue, if found, and that, of course, would be Patrick Twilliger."

Katie stood. "Why would she leave such important details to him? She didn't even know Patrick before the other day. And, from what Helen told me, I was supposed to get a lot more than a hundred thousand."

Scott took off his reading glasses. "First, Helen always hoped she'd find out what became of her son. And, even if that didn't happen during her lifetime, she hoped she'd be close to him in death. Second, the stipulation on death was included because there was some messiness when her father died. As to the amount, that was Helen's decision."

I turned to James and choked out. "Do you mind if I grab water?"

"It's your house, bro. Have at it."

My mouth dropped. *My house?* I guess it was. "Anyone else want something?"

In unison, they said, "Water."

I walked into the half-bath and splashed my face. It was so much money. And, to get left this house, this incredible house. I dried off, walked to the living room, and grabbed several cold-water bottles. Patty took them from me when I returned and handed them around.

Scott lifted the bottle to his lips, drank, and put it down. "I'll courier copies to each of you and will be in close contact as we close out Helen's estate. If you have any questions, please don't hesitate to call. Helen was not just a client; she was a good friend, and I shall miss her." He gathered the papers, put them in his briefcase, and left.

The room was silent for a moment. Then James said, "I'll get my things from my room and clear out."

I shook my head. "Don't be silly."

Katie stood and almost walked past me. She stopped. "I know we got off to a rough start, but I loved Helen. I hope you'll let me help in planning her final rest."

I said, "I'd like that."

Katie left.

I stretched. "Let's go into the living room."

"You two should check out of the hotel and stay here." James plopped down on the sofa.

"How many bedrooms are in this place?" Patty sat next to me.

"Five. All with their own bathrooms."

Patty shrugged. "I guess we should move our stuff. No sense paying a hotel bill if it's not necessary."

A tall woman in her sixties with her hair in a severe bun walked into the room, accompanied by a shorter, more casually dressed forty-ish woman with short brown hair. The taller one extended her hand. "I'm Matilda, the cook. You must be Patrick. Helen was so happy these last few days."

I stood and shook her hand. "Nice to meet you."

The other woman stepped forward. "Louisa. I clean the house. Philippe, my husband, takes care of the grounds. He'll be back later."

Matilda cleared her throat. "I worked for Helen for the last fifteen years. She was a great employer."

I introduced Patty to them both.

James retrieved another bottle of water. "Patrick and Patty will be moving into the Peyote room later today. Would you please make sure it's ready for them?"

Matilda shuffled her feet. "James, what would you like me to serve for dinner tonight? Will Patrick and Patty be joining you?"

James laughed and pointed at me. "It's Patrick's house now. Ask him. One thing you should know, he's not a fan of spice."

Patty squirmed, and her face flushed. "We're not used to having a cook, and I'm not sure what you have in the fridge. We're okay with a little spice. Just not five-alarm kind of spice. Matilda, why don't you surprise us?"

"Very well." She and Louisa left the room.

I sat back in the chair. "This is going to take getting used to. A cook, a maid, and a gardener. Very different from home."

The doorbell rang. I strode down the corridor and opened the door. Two men in rumpled brown suits stood under the arch. I asked, "Can I help you?"

The beefier one held out identification. "Lieutenant Muniz and this is Detective Schwartz. May we come in?"

"Of course." I led them to the living room and introduced them to James and Patty. "What's this about?"

"May I ask what your relationship is to Helen McGregor?"

"Son and step-son." James pointed to me and then himself.

"My wife." I put my hand on Patty's shoulder. "What's this all about?"

"Helen McGregor was murdered."

Patty gasped. "What? That's horrible."

"We'll need to have all of you come to the station for questioning." The Lieutenant gestured toward the door. "Now."

"You can't think one of us did it." James blanched.

"We're trying to get some facts established."

"Do we need an attorney?"

"You're not being arrested. We just have some questions."

* * *

I was led to one of the rooms in the police station for questioning, James to another, and Patty to another. I sat on the cold steel chair, and Detective Schwartz soon joined me. "Let's get started. You are Helen McGregor's son?"

"That's correct."

"And, you just met her?"

"I met her for the first time two nights before she was killed."

His eyebrow rose.

"I was adopted and recently learned who she was and that she was still alive," I explained about the DNA test.

"You have to admit, it is suspicious. You two meet, and then she's murdered. Mrs. McGregor's attorney told us you inherited her house, a household account, and a million dollars free and clear. Sounds like motive to me."

"But I didn't even know I was in her will. She talked about changing it the night she died, but she didn't have enough time to do it. Besides, I wasn't even staying with her. I dropped her off at the house and went back to the hotel. She died at night. I wasn't there."

"Is there anyone who can vouch for that?"

I groaned. "No. I was alone. My wife hadn't arrived yet."

"Uh-huh."

"I want an attorney." I squirmed. "I'm not going to answer any questions until I have counsel." I wrung my hands. How had this gone so wrong? All I wanted to do was meet my mother. Now she was dead, and I was in a police interrogation room.

An hour later, a gentleman with white hair and spectacles hurried into the room. He shook my hand. "Your wife hired me to represent you."

"How did she know who to call?"

"Helen's attorney recommended me."

"I didn't kill Helen."

* * *

We returned to the house at eight. The dining room table was set for three. I sank into one of the seats, and James objected, "You should sit at the head of the table."

"Who cares at this point? Sit."

He sat across from me, and Patty sat in the disputed seat. "What a day."

I poured wine and took a long sip. "This is good."

"Helen has a great cellar. Had." James grimaced. "What a mess."

Matilda presented dinner. "I made one of my favorite chicken and rice dishes. Chicken, black beans, zucchini, corn, and tomatoes. Enjoy. Leave the dishes in the sudsy water in the sink; I'll attend to them tomorrow." She left.

Patty passed the salad bowl. I took a large helping and then passed my plate for the chicken. She heaped my plate.

"I've had this before. It's good." James took the plate.

"This is heaven," Patty sniffed. "Cumin and maybe coriander. Ooh and lime. I love the lime."

We were silent as we dug in, then Patty said, "Once they realized I got here after the murder, they let me go. I was able to check out of the hotel, bring our stuff here, and get back in time to pick you both up. Why on earth did they have you there so long?"

I put a handful of tortilla chips on my plate. "No alibi."

James shrugged. "Me either. At least you weren't staying here."

"That didn't seem to matter to them. They didn't even seem to care that I didn't know I would inherit anything."

"Oh, I don't know about that. After the police talked to you, they talked to me. When they found out how much I inherited, they asked what happened at the dinner the other night. I told them I behaved like a child when Helen told me she was changing her will, and I stalked off."

68

Patty moved the food around on her plate with her fork. "I know it's none of my business, but what did you inherit?"

"Right around twenty-mill."

Patty's mouth dropped.

"Yep. I think I'm now suspect numero uno."

CHAPTER 11

Patrick

I didn't sleep well. It seemed surreal that the police would think I had murdered my mother. It was hard for me to kill spiders that the kids found in their rooms.

Patty lifted her head and turned toward me. "I thought you were awake. You tossed and turned all night. Hopefully, you got a little shut-eye."

"Not much. What are we going to do?"

"I'm going to call Merry. She knows this stuff." Patty grabbed her phone from the side table and pressed speaker.

"What's up?" Merry answered.

"I need you here."

"What? In Phoenix? Why?"

"We found out last night that Helen was killed."

"Killed? That's awful."

"Patrick's under suspicion and they're breathing down his brother's neck too. Look at all the murderers you helped catch. Patrick's on the phone too." Patty sat on the edge of the bed, next to me.

"I'm so sorry about your mother, Patrick."

I said, "Thank you. I know it's a lot to ask, but you may be able to help. This is all so new to us."

"That was here, in Hopeful. I know everyone. They talk to me. Besides, I'm still working out stuff with Jenny."

Patty said, "You won't be leaving her alone. She can stay at my house with my parents."

"But, I have to take her on trips to see schools."

"That's not till August." Patty reminded her.

Merry groaned.

"Who's your best friend?"

"You."

"And who needs you?"

She groaned again. "You."

"I'll send you an e-ticket." Patty pressed end, and her fingers worked the phone.

There was a soft knock, so I tossed on a robe and pulled the door open. Louisa stepped past me with a tray and placed it on the small table near the dresser. My face flushed. "Umm. Thanks. You don't have to go to all this trouble."

"It's my job."

"Oh. Hmm. Okay."

"Matilda wants to know what time you'd like breakfast."

I checked my phone. "Eight-thirty? Is that too late? We could be ready earlier."

"Whenever you want. You're the boss." She gave me a strange look and shut the door behind her.

I handed Patty a cup of coffee and the small pitcher of cream. "This is going to take some getting used to."

Patty stirred cream in the cup until it reached a deep mocha color. "It does feel weird, but on the other hand, someone just delivered coffee to my room."

"I feel guilty about asking Merry to come all the way here." I sat next to Patty on the bed.

"Who else do we know who has experience with murders?"

"Every time she's involved in a case, she's almost killed."

Patty's face flushed. "It won't happen this time. We'll be here. She'll get to the bottom of this, and we'll keep her safe."

I sighed. "What time does Merry's plane arrive?"

"Seven."

"Rob won't be happy we're getting her involved in this."

"I know."

I folded the paper and put it on the bed. "We have about thirty minutes till breakfast."

"Good. Then we have time for a quick shower."

* * *

Matilda made Huevos Rancheros with warmed tortillas and served them on the patio by the pool. "Going to be a scorcher. Let me know if you need anything else."

James passed the coffee to Patty, and she filled her cup. "It looks delicious."

He shook hot sauce over everything on his plate. "It is."

"How can you eat that? My stomach lining would give out." I eyed the glistening red dots and frowned.

"If you eat spicy food, you won't feel the heat as much." James shoveled the doctored eggs into his mouth.

Patty sipped coffee. "What time are we supposed to be at the funeral home?"

"Ten-thirty. We have time." James nudged me. "Did you invite Katie? Don't forget, she's our local connection. She knows the people to invite and what Helen wanted."

"I texted her last night. She said she'd be there. Do you want to drive together? Or separately?" I retrieved an English muffin from the center of the table and spread a liberal amount of strawberry jam on it.

James said, "May as well go together. What would you say to lunch out afterward? I know a place that's not too far from town."

"Sounds good." I added, "By the way, a friend of Patty's is coming to stay with us."

James's eyebrow rose. "Strange time to be having friends. It's hot as blazes, and we're still trying to figure out what happened to Helen."

Patty rose and rubbed the blue and white tile at the edge of the pool. "She's helped the police in our small town solve several murders. You met her at my house for dinner, Merry March."

"I'm sure the detectives would be happy to have her help." James laughed.

Patty walked back to the table. "This is serious. She can help, and she's coming."

James shrugged and rose. "The more, the merrier. I'll be down by ten-fifteen." He walked toward his room.

"Where's Merry going to sleep? I better get a room ready," Patty said.

Matilda walked out to the pool with a tray and began to clear the dishes.

I cleared my throat. "Um. Matilda, if it's not too much trouble, we're going to have another guest for dinner. Actually, she'll be staying with us for a few days."

"Which room would you like her to stay in?" Matilda continued to load dishes on the tray.

"I, uh, really don't know. Definitely not Helen's."

"There's a nice one with a queen bed and view of the pool." She pointed at French doors with a small balcony to the left on the second floor.

Patty said, "That would be perfect. Do you know where the sheets are? I'll make it up this morning."

"Louisa will do that."

"It's no trouble; I can do it before we leave." Patty handed Matilda her coffee mug.

Matilda placed it on the tray and straightened her spine. "Did Louisa do something wrong?"

"Not at all," I interjected.

"Good. I'll tell her to make up the room. Is there anything special you'd like for dinner?"

Patty sank onto her chair. "Scallops at eight-thirty."

"Very well." Matilda lifted the tray, maneuvered through the door to the kitchen, and shut it behind her.

"This is going to take some getting used to." Patty put her head in her hands.

* * *

My stomach twisted as we drove to the funeral home. I hoped we wouldn't have a repeat of the previous day. I tried to focus on the drive, but my eye wandered to the cactus in bloom along the roadway. They provided dots of color and gave relief to the earthen brown of the landscape. Maybe everything would be okay.

James made small talk about the Cardinals as I maneuvered the car into a parking spot, and we got out. Katie waited for us by the door, and we walked inside together.

"I have to say, I'm becoming a big fan of air conditioning," Patty said.

Katie laughed.

The funeral director greeted us. "The police called. They'll be releasing the body sometime tomorrow. Have you decided what you want to do?"

Katie nodded toward me. "He's in charge."

I sighed. "I thought you made good points yesterday. Let's talk this through. Neither James nor I live here, and you know who all her friends are."

The funeral director pointed to a small conference room. "Why don't you get comfortable in there, and I'll bring cold water? Unless someone would like a soda?"

"Any hard liquor?" James asked.

Patty's mouth opened—

"Just kidding. Water is fine."

The room included an oversized table that had seen better days along with wooden chairs that almost touched the walls. The carpet was worn, drab brown, and the overall ambiance was as depressing as the reason for us being there. James and I squeezed through to the furthermost seats, and Katie and Patty took the ones closest to where the funeral director had set up his folders.

He returned with bottles of water, handed them out, and sat. "I understand that yesterday there was some discussion of the beautiful cherrywood casket with rose liner."

Katie smiled. "It was lovely. It's just what Helen would have wanted."

I shifted in my seat. "I don't disagree. My concern is two-fold. First, it's so nice I can't bear to think of burning such artisanship. Second, it's expensive, and I feel like we'd be throwing away Helen's hard-earned cash. I'd rather donate to a charity for that amount because it'd do more good."

"If I may—" the funeral director interjected. "It may sound a little strange, but have you thought about renting a coffin?"

"Renting? That means it's used. I don't know how I feel about that." Katie shuddered.

"It's fairly straightforward and is becoming more accepted, with so many people opting for cremation. You can rent the cherrywood casket, and use it for any public viewings. Then when it's time for the cremation, we move Helen to a plain pine box. Please be assured we perform a thorough cleaning of the rentals between clients."

I moved my chair closer to the table. "I like it. Provided the cost is right."

The funeral director went through the options and costs. Katie reached for the paper listing the terms, and as she did, her sleeve slid down her arm, revealing a red, blistering streak.

James asked, "What happened to your arm?"

"Sunburn. You'd think a Phoenix native would know how to apply sunscreen." She tugged her sleeve back in place and handed the sheet to James.

He glanced at it. "Patrick's right. We should rent."

I turned toward Katie. "I know this isn't quite what you had in mind, but I do think it's the best solution. If you don't mind, since you know everyone, I'd like you to plan the public viewing."

"I'd like that." Katie smiled. "I know just what Helen would have wanted, and who to invite."

We stood and shook the funeral director's hand.

* * *

James and I were relaxing in the Jacuzzi when Patty walked out, purse in hand. I stood. "I didn't realize it was so late. I'll get dressed."

"Hang out with James. I can pick-up Merry on my own."

I sank back into the swirling water. "Don't have to tell me twice."

"Isn't it too hot for that?"

"Not when you alternate between the pool and spa." I smiled.

Matilda carried beers in an ice-filled bucket and a tray of assorted olives, and cured meats. She set the nibbles and bucket down on the wrought-iron table. "Let me know if you need anything else."

Patty speared an olive. "Looks like you're in good hands. I'll be back."

"This is the life." I let the spa jets massage my lower back.

James leaped from the hot tub and grabbed a beer. He lifted it. "Want one?"

I nodded, and he handed it to me as he sank back into the spa. "Remind me to show you how the security system and cameras work before we go to bed tonight."

"Helen had cameras?"

"Spread like this? You betcha." He took a long pull on his beer.

CHAPTER 12

Merry

It was a mad dash to the airport, between giving last-minute instructions at work and getting Jenny squared away with Patty's parents. I barely had time to give Rob a quick kiss before rushing through security. I found my seat, stowed my carry-on, and pulled out my book. At least I'd have uninterrupted reading time.

After we landed, I wove past the travelers that seemed to stop in the middle of the concourse for no reason. I maneuvered down the escalator to baggage claim and spied Patty waving her arms.

A few moments later, she enveloped me in a hug. "Thanks for coming."

"I deserve major friend points."

"That you do. Let's get your luggage."

I motioned toward my roller bag. "This is it."

Her eyebrow rose.

"I pack efficiently."

We drove to the house in relative silence, punctuated only by my occasional exclamation about the flat terrain and blooming bougainvillea. When we pulled into the driveway, my jaw dropped. "You told me it was big, but I had no idea. This place is huge. And, so pretty. I love the tiled roof."

Patty took my suitcase from the car and rolled it toward the garage. Patrick greeted us, took the bag from her, and gave me a quick hug. "Merry, thank you for coming. Dinner's in a half hour. Let me show you your room."

He carried the bag up the massive mahogany staircase and walked to the left. Three doors down, he opened one onto a lovely room featuring a large bed with what looked to be a crocheted canopy. French doors led to a small balcony overlooking the pool area.

I said, "Thanks, Patrick. I'll be down in a few minutes." He left.

"And, now for the bathroom," Patty quipped. She opened the door, and I gasped.

"I love the tub. And, the shower. And, look at these hammered copper sinks." I grabbed Patty's arm. "This place is beautiful. I can't believe it's all yours."

"Me either. I better leave you alone, or we'll be late for dinner."

I eyed the tub.

"You better not. You have exactly—" She checked her watch "—eight minutes till dinner. And, Matilda's serving scallops."

I pushed her out the door. "I'll be there."

* * *

I walked into the dining room. Both men jumped to their feet, and James pulled out my chair. "Merry, it's good to see you again."

I extended my hand. "I'm sorry about your step-mother."

"Thanks."

I sat at the other end of the table from Patty, and James retook his seat opposite his half-brother.

Matilda came into the room carrying a large platter. "This is dirty rice, with sausage and chicken livers. It's topped with just-seared scallops. I'll be right back with a salad and dinner rolls."

"So this is how the other half lives." My eyes widened.

Patrick poured wine and lifted his glass. "Thanks, Merry, for braving the Phoenix heat to help us."

"I'm starving. I must have looked pitiful on the plane because the flight attendant gave me two bags of peanuts." I leaned forward toward the platter, cupping my hand and waving it toward my face. "The onions and peppers smell wonderful."

Matilda returned and set the salad and rolls on the table. "There's cheesecake in the refrigerator if you save room for dessert, and fresh coffee is brewing. I'll see you in the morning." She left.

We dug in like we hadn't eaten for weeks. After dinner, Patrick poured coffee, and Patty cut the mocha cheesecake with a chocolate, graham cracker crust.

I took a bite. "It would be helpful if you told me exactly what happened that last night. Who wants to start?"

James cleared his throat. "I'll go. I had business downtown during the day and met Patrick and Helen at the restaurant. It started pleasantly enough; then, Helen started talking about changing her will. I'm embarrassed now, but I got pretty hot. I've been my dad's only child my whole life. And, the thought of someone else sharing in what I thought would be mine hit me the wrong way." He sipped coffee. "Sorry, bro."

"What happened next?" I swirled cream into the coffee.

"I stalked away like a two-year-old. I drove back to the house, slammed a few doors, and did about twenty laps in the pool. While I was swimming, I realized how stupid I'd been. I was given the incredible gift of a brother, and here I was, acting like a jackass over more money than I'll probably spend in my lifetime. I toweled off, took a shower, and changed. I heard Helen in the kitchen, so I went to apologize. She was nice about it, hugged me, and said she was going to email her lawyer to get him started on the paperwork.

"I played video games in the cabana till late. Then I went to bed and woke to Louisa screaming Helen was dead." He shuddered and choked out, "I couldn't believe it. I ran to her room and felt for a pulse. There was nothing I could do; she was gone."

Patty clasped James's hand and squeezed it.

I turned to Patrick. "Are you ready?"

"Not much to tell. Helen and I finished dinner, and I drove her home. I was going to come in but thought it would be better if she spoke with James alone. I drove back to the hotel and called Patty." Patrick's face grew red.

Patty leaned toward him. "Are you okay? We could leave this till morning."

"I'm good. Carry on." He sipped his coffee.

"How did you find out she died?"

James raised his hand. "I called him."

Patrick nodded.

"This is depressing. Let's have an after-dinner drink by the pool. It should be cool enough now." James stood.

I said, "Patty, and I will put the dishes in the sink and meet you outside."

Patty retrieved a tray, and we piled the dessert plates on it. She nudged my arm. "What did you think?"

"I'm pretty sure Patrick didn't kill her, but that means someone else did. His brother was in the house, and he stood to gain a lot. Who else could have done it?"

"That's what we need to find out. I pray it wasn't James."

There was the faintest glow, signaling the coming dawn. I stretched and decided to go in search of coffee. I donned shorts, t-shirt, and flip flops and wandered down the stairs. The faint scent of java hit my nostrils. *Someone's already made coffee.* I was in Heaven. I walked into the kitchen, and a full carafe beckoned me. I filled a mug.

Matilda stood at the marble-topped counter, rolling dough. "You're up early."

"Time change. May I join you?" She nodded, and I sat at the island, watching her practiced hands work. "What are you making?"

"Pastries. I thought I'd do a few cheese, some cherry, and a couple of cinnamon swirl." She eyed me. "They won't be ready for another hour or so. If you're hungry, I have bagels in the freezer."

"I can wait." I sipped coffee and took in the kitchen. "I'm jealous of the stove. It looks top of the line."

Her gaze wandered the room. "Helen had the kitchen redone about eight years ago, and she asked me to help design it. I have a proofing drawer, large pantry, double oven, and an eight burner stove."

"I love to bake, but I'm not at your level. I mostly bake for people around town."

"I've been doing this for a long time, professionally." Matilda smiled. "It's good to have a fellow baker in the house. So many people don't understand the precision it involves."

"If your baking matches the level of the cooking you did last night, I'm going to be ten pounds heavier when I leave."

She chuckled.

"How long did you work for Helen?"

"Fifteen years. I had my work cut out for me. When Frank was alive, they had big events every month. After he died, she cut back. The only large gala she threw lately was a benefit for the theatre. That was Katie's doing. Even though she has her issues, I guess I'm glad she got Helen back out into civilization."

"Don't you like Katie?"

"It's not for me to like or dislike any of Helen's friends." She sniffed. "Look at me. Chattering away instead of focusing on the pastries. People will be coming down hungry, and nothing will be ready. Why don't you sit by the pool and relax?"

Getting the message, I moved away from the table, freshened my cup, and walked out to the pool. I had pushed too hard. *Note to self: try subtlety.*

I sat by the side of the pool and dangled my feet in the water. *I could get used to this. Great coffee and fresh pastry.* I texted Jenny: "How are things going?"

"Busy. Your office is partially painted. Hope you like chartreuse."

I called her. "You didn't really paint it lime green?"

"I used the boring light grey you left me. Cindy and Jacob helped, and we should have it all done tomorrow."

"I'm sure it will look great. Thanks."

"Not like I had a choice," she grumbled.

"Either way, I appreciate it. I love you."

There was a pause, and then she said, "Me too."

I hit end.

Patty sat down next to me. "The water feels so good."

"It does. Matilda's not a big Katie fan."

Patty arched a brow. "And, how did you find out that little tidbit?"

"Early bird gets the worm and all that. Or at least fresh coffee. Matilda was fairly low-key about it, but there's a story there."

"There's something off about Katie. I guess I'm not a big fan either." Patty kicked her feet.

"Hey, watch the splashing. You saw how small my suitcase was."

"Sorry. I'll try to control myself. You'll get a chance to meet her at lunch today. She's coming by to talk about the memorial service."

"I thought Patrick was in charge of that?"

"He is." She shrugged. "Olive branch."

* * *

After breakfast, I returned to my room for a book. Louisa was making the bed. I pulled up the sheet. "Let me help."

"No need. It's my job."

I continued to work on one side. "The gardens are lovely."

She beamed. "My husband, Philippe, works hard. It's a lot to take care of, but he keeps everything so tidy."

"I'm impressed with people who can sculpt bushes. When I try with mine back home, they always look hacked."

"He'd be happy to give you tips." She smoothed the bedspread. "I was going to do your bathroom next, but would you like me to come back later?"

"I was just getting my book." I picked it up from the night table. "I heard you found Helen. That must have been horrible."

"It was. She was laying there, arm half off the bed, and a pillow on the floor." Her eyes darted, and her hand rose to her mouth. "I...I didn't tell the police about the pillow being on the floor. I put it back on the bed because I didn't want them to think I was a sloppy housekeeper."

I nodded. "I'm sure that seemed like the right thing to do at the moment, but you need to call the detective and tell him about it. Now we know Helen was murdered; every detail is important."

She shivered. "I can't believe someone murdered her. It can't be somebody here. Maybe it was a break-in."

"How many people have keys to the house?"

"I'm not sure." She stared at the ceiling. "There's Matilda, me, Philippe, and of course, James." She paused. "Oh, and now Patrick and Patty, of course."

"Did Patrick have a key before she was murdered?"

"I couldn't say for sure, but I don't think so because I saw James give him a key after the lawyer came." She walked toward the bathroom. "I better get on with it."

"One more thing. Did Helen sleep with her bedroom door locked?"

Louisa shook her head. "It was never locked when I brought coffee in the morning. I guess she could have locked it and then unlocked it when she got up, but sometimes she was still sleeping when I came in."

I left, book in hand, strolling toward the pool. When I opened the door, the heat hit me like a brick wall. Deciding to stay in the air conditioning, I wandered past the living room into the library. It was a cozy place with dark brown leather chairs and tons of books lining the shelves. My finger ran across the spines. *Someone was an Agatha Christie fan.* I settled in one of the armchairs and put my feet on the ottoman.

Patty called, "Merry?"

"In here."

She plopped onto the chair next to me. "It figures I'd find you in the library."

"I was surprised you weren't already in here."

"Touché. Katie will be here in about thirty minutes."

"Can't wait to meet her."

"I talked to my mom. The kids haven't set the house on fire yet, and they are enjoying Grandma's cooking. She said Cindy and Jenny have both been great. They helped the littler ones make ice pops last night. The kids wanted to eat them this morning before camp, but Grandma held the line and told them they'd have to wait till they got home."

"I'm sure their instructors were glad they didn't have all that sugar."

"Cereal's not much better. Plus, it might give them extra marching energy."

A tall, blonde-haired woman strode past the door. Patty called out, "Katie?"

She came back. "Hi, Patty."

"I'm sorry. I didn't hear the doorbell."

"I didn't ring it."

There was an awkward pause. I said, "Oh. You have a key."

"Maybe I should get it back now." Patty held out her hand.

Katie's face reddened, and she pulled her key chain from her purse. She struggled to remove a key. Once it was free, she dropped it into Patty's hand. "Here."

"I'll text Patrick and James to let them know you've arrived."

"I've heard so much about you, but we haven't been introduced. My name is Merry March." I held out my hand, and she shook it.

"Good to meet you." We walked into the living room, and Katie sank onto the sofa across from Patty and pulled a folder from her case. "I've got the plans for Patrick and James to take a look at."

I sat next to Patty, as James and Patrick rounded the corner. Patrick said, "Thanks for pulling this together, Katie. I appreciate it."

James echoed, "Me too."

Katie handed copies of her plan to James, Patrick, and Patty. She turned to me and shrugged. "I'm sorry; I didn't know you'd be here."

I waved my hand. "I'll just follow along on Patty's." There was a spreadsheet of events and then a multi-page attachment of what must have been the names of everyone in Phoenix.

Patrick's eyes widened. "That's a lot of people."

"Helen was a very important part of the community. There are expectations." Katie sighed. "I guess we could cut some of them. I thought we'd have the reception after the memorial back here."

I coughed. "It's none of my business, of course, but would you be expecting Matilda to cater?"

"Of course. She's always done it before." She sat straighter in her chair.

Patty leaned forward. "I think Merry's trying to say if Matilda cooks and Louisa has to clean, they wouldn't be guests, and Helen was important to them as well."

"They're servants," she huffed.

"They are employees. And, they are employees who were close to Helen."

"They weren't that close." Katie's eyes shifted to the door.

Matilda glowered from the opening. "Luncheon is ready." She swiveled and stalked away.

"Oops." Katie gave a nervous titter.

Patrick stood. "Let's go over the rest of this in the dining room."

We filed out, and everyone sat at the table. Matilda ferried in two broccoli and cheese quiches, a large bowl of salad, and assorted rolls. She plopped them on the table and retreated to the kitchen.

Patrick laid a pat of butter on his plate. "We'll have the reception here, but we will hire catering staff to cook, set up, serve, and clean. Katie, can you suggest a company or should I research one?"

"I'll handle it."

We went through the rest of the details and were in agreement with most of her suggestions. Katie told us that Helen always loved Vivaldi's "Four Seasons," so we decided on "Winter" for the beginning of the mass and "On Eagle's Wings" by Michael Joncas, for the recessional. Patrick and James picked the readings they wanted, and we finished lunch on a good note.

"I'll find a caterer today and will come back later with a suggested menu." Katie gathered her papers and left.

"We'll bring the dishes in and talk to Matilda." Patrick jerked his head, and James joined him.

"What did you think of Katie?" Patty sipped iced tea.

"Servants? It's a good thing she didn't inherit the house; I don't think they would have stayed long with her."

* * *

Patty and Patrick took me shopping in downtown Scottsdale. They picked up a few trinkets for the kids, and I found a beautiful blanket for Rob and pretty turquoise earrings for Jenny.

Patrick's phone rang, and he answered. "Uh-huh. Oh. Will do." He pressed end.

"What's up?" Patty touched his arm.

"That was my lawyer. The police want to question me again. I have to meet him there at four."

"I wonder if they want to talk with James too." I followed them back to the car.

CHAPTER 13

Patrick

My lawyer was waiting outside the station, and I shook his hand. "You should have gone in."

He smiled. "Wanted to talk to you out here—the same drill as before. Wait a beat before you answer the question. That gives me a chance to interject if I don't want you to answer."

I nodded. We entered, and Detective Schwartz gestured toward one of the interview rooms. I walked in first, my lawyer next, then the detective. The room contained the same uncomfortable chairs and matching table. My hands began to sweat, and I checked to make sure no leg irons lurked.

My lawyer opened his notepad. "It's been a busy day, so why don't we get started?"

The detective leaned over the table. "Fine. The medical examiner came back with a cause of death. Mrs. McGregor was suffocated."

I sat back in my chair as if shoved. "Suffocated?"

"We believe her pillow was used."

"How awful." I squirmed. "Who would do such a thing?"

"Let's go back to your statement."

"Yes?" I leaned forward.

"You said you dropped Mrs. McGregor off at her house and did not return that evening."

"That's correct."

"Then how do you explain the fact someone saw your car parked outside her house later that evening?"

My lawyer held up his hand. "Give us a moment alone, please."

"Certainly." Detective Schwartz smirked as he left.

"Were you outside Helen's house later that night?"

I dropped my head to my hands. "Yes."

"Why didn't you tell me? Do you know how bad this looks?"

"The houses where Helen lives are so far apart. I didn't think anyone saw me. It's silly. And I was only there for fifteen minutes, maybe less. I didn't go in. I didn't even go to the door." I groaned. "I know it's stupid I didn't tell anyone, but it's embarrassing."

He faced me. "What were you doing there?"

"I was annoyed. My brother had made such a big deal about the inheritance, and there he was, staying in her house. He was closer to her than me, and I was her son."

The lawyer tilted his head.

"My whole life might have been different. I would have been with my actual parents."

Silence.

"It's not as if I didn't love my adoptive parents. They were great. Very encouraging but knew when to get tough with me." I smiled. "My mom can be so funny. She's always playing practical jokes. There was one time—"

"You didn't go in?"

"No. But now I sure wish I had. Maybe I could have saved her." I shifted my weight, trying to make myself more comfortable on the steel chair. "At any rate, I decided you can't change history. I put the car in drive and returned to the hotel."

"I wish you told me this before. It's never good when the police think you've held out on them." The lawyer opened the door and waved.

Detective Schwartz returned with two sodas. He lifted them, and I nodded. My lawyer shook his head, so the Detective popped open the other one. He took a long sip. "Ready to talk?"

My lawyer leaned forward. "Yes."

* * *

The Detective rubbed his forehead. "So, you want me to believe you came back to the house but didn't go inside."

"It's the truth. Helen had a security system with cameras. That should back me up."

"What cameras? I didn't see any cameras. And nobody mentioned them." Detective Schwartz's right eyebrow rose.

"Helen had a security system with cameras in the front."

"None in the back?"

"James told me she thought they'd be too intrusive by the pool."

The Detective wrote a note. "Why didn't you tell me about them before?"

I shrugged. "I thought you knew. When Patty and I moved from the hotel, James showed me how it worked."

* * *

Patty picked me up outside the police station, and I sank onto the passenger seat. "I'm getting tired of this place."

"Me too. What did they want?" She pulled away from the curb.

"Let's go for a drink." She drove for a while, and I pointed to a restaurant on the right. "That place looks good."

She parked. "I'll text Merry, so she doesn't worry." Her fingers flew on the phone, and then she dropped it in her purse. "Let's go."

The bar was dark after being in the relentless sun, and it was old-school, with scarred wooden tables and black leather booths. Patty slid into one side of one and me the other. We both ordered frozen margaritas with salt on the rim.

She clicked her glass to mine. "To better days."

"Someone saw my car outside Helen's late the night she died," I blurted.

"They were mistaken, weren't they?"

"Let me explain." I told her why I went back to Helen's.

"Do you wish you had grown up here?" Patty swirled the half straw in her drink. "We wouldn't have met each other."

I pulled her hand to my lips and kissed it. "We would have always met. And, I would have always fallen for you."

"But all this: the house, the million dollars. You would have had such a different life. Maybe you would have chosen someone better."

I stood, slid onto Patty's side of the booth, and enveloped her in a hug. "There's no one better than you. I love the life I've led, and look forward to growing old with you. I was just so angry at the moment. And jealous. That's why I went back to her house. Now my only regret is Helen didn't get a chance to meet you. And the kids." I kissed her. "She would have adored you."

✵ ✵ ✵

The police were taking discs from the security system when we returned to the house. James said, "They had a warrant. Why did they want to talk to you?"

"Later." Patty and I strolled into the living room, and James followed. Merry wandered in from the pool with a robe on and a towel wrapped around her head.

Patty said, "Isn't it too hot to be by the pool?"

Merry laughed. "Maybe 'by the pool,' but certainly not 'in the pool.' I'll be back down in ten." She raced up the steps.

We sat there silently, hearing the police banging around as they gathered the discs. Detective Schwartz walked into the room. "We're taking them all." His eyes met mine. "You're sure Helen didn't have cameras in the back?"

"Not to my knowledge." I turned to James.

"She didn't the last time I was down, which would have been in early spring."

"We'll be going now. Don't anyone leave town." The door slammed.

Patty jumped. "I want this to be over."

I hugged her. "So do I; So do I."

Matilda walked into the living room. "It's time for me to leave. There's a roast in the oven on warm, salad in the refrigerator, and fresh rolls on the table. I wasn't sure what time you'd want to eat with all that's been going on."

I stood. "Thanks, Matilda. We're sorry to have kept you. Hopefully, things will calm down soon."

She walked back through the door to the kitchen.

James retrieved a bottle of white wine. "It's been a day. Anyone for a splash?"

I walked over for a glass. "Patty?"

She shook her head. "Not so soon after that margarita. Maybe at dinner."

Merry joined us, took the glass I held out to her and sank onto the sofa next to Patty. "So, what happened? Why did they need to see Patrick again? And why were they here?"

I sat facing them. "I'm embarrassed to say."

James plopped down next to me, and I told them.

Merry tsked. "It's never a good idea to hold out on the police."

"I know. I just didn't think anyone would find out. I feel so silly."

James laughed. "Don't worry about it, bro. First, it takes the heat off me. And, second, it makes me feel a little better about blowing up at dinner the other night. I guess jealousy is just a human condition."

"What was your childhood like, James?" Merry sat back on the sofa and tucked her foot underneath her.

"Strange."

Patty said, "How so?"

"It was pretty normal till Helen came along. A Dad who worked all the time, plus a mom who also worked but always had dinner on the table by six. A regular Ozzie and Harriet existence. Then all of a sudden, bye-bye dad, move to a smaller house, and a bitter mom who never baked another birthday cake for me to this day."

I nudged James. "Birthday cake?"

"I told you he left when I was eight. It was actually on my birthday. Mom made my favorite cake. Chocolate with chocolate frosting and rainbow sprinkles. It was the last one I had, and I ate it by myself in a dark kitchen."

"That's so sad," Merry said.

"It was horrible. I kept thinking something I did caused him to go. Twenty years, several rounds of counseling, and an ex-wife later, I realized it wasn't me. It was always about Helen. She had a Mata Hari-like hold on him.

"When we moved to the small house, I had to change schools. He hadn't come to my baseball games before because he was always too busy, but after the split, it felt like he was just avoiding me. Once a few years had passed, he became more involved, but, to be honest, I never really forgave him. Or her."

Merry leaned forward. "Your mother?"

He shook his head. "Helen. She ruined our lives."

"But you stayed close to her after your father died. Why would you do that if she caused you so much pain?" Patty took a few peanuts from a dish on the coffee table.

"Look at this place. When I came on school breaks, I was treated like a king. No small two bedrooms here. Helen was nice to me, and they made sure I had all the latest games to play while I was here. No way was I going to jinx a good thing.

"Then later, after Dad died, it made sense to stay in touch. Helen missed him and was generous with her money. It sounds bad, but I figured I was her only heir. For the potential reward, it wasn't too difficult to have her fawn over me." James clapped me on the shoulder. "Who knew there was another kid who'd enter the picture so near the end?"

I rubbed my arms. "James, you know my reaching out was never about the money. I wanted to get to know my mother."

"I'm sorry you're not going to get to do that."

"Me too. And, I'm sorry Helen and Frank were the cause of so much pain in your life."

"Apology accepted. Who's up for dinner?"

I lay in bed with Patty. She leaned on one elbow and looked me straight in the eyes. "You think he killed her?"

"Evidence is piling up. James was in the house, wasn't happy she was changing her will, and didn't tell the police about the camera surveillance."

"How does not telling the police about the recordings benefit James?"

I drew her closer. "Because they'll see I didn't stay. And, they'll see no one else came. That means whoever killed her was in the house."

CHAPTER 14

Merry

By six the next morning, I was propped up near the French press, watching the coffee's slow, tortuous drip to the carafe below. Patty walked into the kitchen, rubbing her eyes, and Matilda said, "I could have the coffee made earlier if this is the time you would like it served."

Patty groaned. "I'm hoping this is a one-off. My happy world starts much later. At least in Phoenix. I got up early so I could talk to the kids. I miss them."

I lifted my face from the cool counter. "Do you have children, Matilda?"

"I never had the pleasure." She continued to put slices of bacon on a rack.

"Pets?" Patty asked.

"Messy things. Hair everywhere." Matilda slid the sheet tray into the oven.

"Husband?"

"Wasn't much better than pets. Was always cleaning up after him." She washed her hands. "Pardon me; I'm going to gather herbs from the garden for breakfast." She strolled out the door.

The last of the water flowed through the coffee beans. Patty grabbed the carafe, poured a full cup, and cradled it as if it were the most precious elixir in the world.

"I was here first." I plucked the carafe from her hand before she could return it to its base.

Patty pushed an errant lock of hair from her face. "Do you think Matilda likes me?"

"I'm sure she does." I poured the cream in my coffee.

"She gives me a weird vibe."

I pushed her arm. "Maybe it's the fact you are now the lady of the house."

Patty looked down at her faded robe, well-used nightie, and flip flops. "Doubtful."

"What'd you think about what James said last night?"

"It was sad. I couldn't imagine it if Dad left my mother for someone else. Plus, his standard of living worsened after his dad left them. No one ever considers the ripples caused in people's lives by one person's selfish actions."

"Maybe what he had with Helen was true love. Maybe his marriage was so bad he needed to get out. Kids aren't always the best judge of what's happening. I know that firsthand."

"Even if it was 'true love,'" Patty air-quoted, "it made an impact on James's life."

I shivered. "What if James wanted revenge?"

"I don't know about revenge, but he certainly wanted the money, and his plan to get it might have been messed up when Patrick arrived."

"Talking about me?" James strode into the room.

I coughed. "Sorry. Coffee went down the wrong way."

"Where's Matilda? Did you chase her off?"

"I'm right here. I thought we'd have omelets with herbs this morning." She held up a bundle as she walked back into the kitchen.

"Looks good to me. I'm starving." James filled his mug and went into the dining room. Patty and I followed. Patrick was sitting at the table, polishing off a cherry Danish.

"When did you come down?" Patty plopped next to Patrick and stole a piece of his Danish.

"About five minutes ago. I was talking to Louisa." He finished the last piece of his pastry.

"She's getting an early start."

"She and Phillipe have some sort of thing this afternoon. They need to leave early. Oh, that reminds me. Phillipe wanted me to know there'd been damage to one of the oleander hedges around the pool." Patrick put another Danish on his plate.

Matilda poked her head through the kitchen door. "It'll be about ten minutes. The bacon's not quite done yet." She shut the door.

"We have time, so let's take a look." Patty grabbed her mug and took the lead. Phillippe was fishing errant leaves from the pool.

Patrick said, "I heard one of the oleanders was damaged?"

"Over here." Phillipe strode to the far right corner of the pool and opened the gate. "You can't see it from this side."

We turned the corner past the blooming fuchsia bougainvillea, beds of multi-colored zinnias, and the purple globe amaranth. He pointed to the oleander shrubs, which were covered in apricot blooms. "See here and here? It's almost like someone squeezed through. There are quite a few broken branches, so I'm going to prune it back and hope it recovers."

Patrick rubbed a broken end. "When did this happen?"

"Not sure. I've been focusing on the desert garden, so I haven't been over on this side for a week or so."

❋ ❋ ❋

"This is the life." I drifted by on a turquoise blue float.

Patty nudged it, sending it spinning toward the deep end. "Don't get too comfortable. We're meeting Katie at the caterer's at one."

"You could have pushed me toward my glass of lemonade."

98

"Next time, I'll work on my aim." Patty sighed. "I wish we had a copy of the discs the police took. I keep wondering if anyone else stopped by the night Helen was killed."

"We do." James handed me my drink from the side of the pool.

"What do you mean?"

"The security company keeps a backup disc, just in case our system goes down."

"Why didn't you tell us that?" I set my lemonade on the side of the pool and launched my lounge toward the shallow end. "Let's go."

"Not so fast, Nancy Drew. The place is over near the airport, and we have to meet Katie in Scottsdale." James strolled back to the table, turned on the misters, and sat.

I climbed out of the pool. "Would you call and ask if they would make a duplicate from a week before Helen's death till today? That way, we could pick it up on the way back."

"It's not really on the way back."

I lifted my eyebrow.

"I'll call." He walked toward the house, passing Patrick. "Demanding women."

"You have no idea." Patrick said, "Patty, you need to get out if we're going to be on time."

She pushed off the side of the pool with her feet, and her pink float careened toward the stairs. "Be with you in a minute."

* * *

The caterer wore a black suit with a severe white blouse and waited as Katie handed us menus. After we sat, Katie said, "Helen loved spice, so I think we should include dishes that are on the hot side. Not screaming hot, just a pleasant heat. Here are samples of what I think we should incorporate."

Patrick squirmed, and James waved him off. "I'll take one for the team."

He and I reached for two of the chicken skewers.

"It's high on the heat-o-meter. I don't think I'd have that again." My eyes ran, and I reached for a glass of water.

"This is good. A bit like biting into a flaming shish kabob, but oddly enough, it's still quite tasty." James smiled. "What's next?"

The caterer lined up several more items. "These are milder canapes. Don't worry; I'll have everything marked; the more peppers, the more heat." She handed Patrick a card, "This is for the one Merry, and James just ate." The card was inscribed Chicken Diablo and had four red cayenne peppers across the bottom.

Patrick said, "This works. I'd know to stay away from that one."

"Is this spanakopita?" Patty pointed to a triangular-shaped phyllo dough wrapped item on the left.

"It's kind of a Mexican-Greek fusion version. It uses cotija cheese versus feta."

"Love that." Patty took a bite. "Sublime."

We tasted the rest of the dishes, finalized the menu, and left the caterer with her notes. Patrick said, "Thanks for arranging this caterer, Katie. I think she's going to do a great job."

"She comes highly recommended. The funeral mass is at eleven, and Matilda will need to vacate the kitchen by eight on Saturday so the caterer's team can do their magic. I've also arranged for extra seating, tents for the pool and garden areas, and misters. Those will be loaded in tomorrow night."

Patrick shook her hand. "Thanks for working so hard. You'll make Helen's memorial a terrific success."

✳ ✳ ✳

Patrick and James slid into the front seats of the car, Patty and I the back. Patty rapped on Patrick's headrest. "Don't forget, we need to stop by the security office."

"Will do." He punched in the street address and started the car.

Fifteen minutes later, Patrick pulled up in front of their offices. James popped his seatbelt. "No need for all of us to go, I'll run in and grab the disc." He hopped out, walked to the door, and disappeared inside.

"Maybe we should have gone with him." I leaned forward.

"He's my brother."

Patty said, "Half."

"Whatever. He had nothing to do with Helen's death." He folded his arms.

James walked out, holding up the disc case. "Success."

After dinner, we adjourned to the movie theater in the wing off the kitchen. It had plush black leather recliners, blackout drapes, a small bar, and a popcorn machine. I sank onto one of the chairs. "This is nice. Too bad, we can't watch a movie."

James put the disc in the computer and connected it to the system. He walked back with the remote and held it out to Patrick. "Want to drive?"

Patrick shook his head. "You got this."

James pressed play, and the grainy front yard appeared. "I hope it's clearer than this."

"Must be at night. Hit fast forward, or this is going to take forever."

During the daytime, the picture was far clearer. "Stop! There's Patrick's rental pulling up."

James hit pause. It was daytime, and Patrick was sitting in his car. Patty grabbed popcorn. "This must have been your first day in Phoenix." Patrick exited and walked toward the door like his feet were made of lead. Patty put her hand in his and squeezed. "You must have been so nervous."

"I was."

He disappeared into the house. Patrick told James, "May as well speed it up; I was there a while."

In what seemed like just a few minutes later, Patrick walked toward the car. A white-haired woman held his arm. As he rounded the corner of the vehicle, the camera caught his broad smile.

"Fast forward again?" James asked.

Patrick nodded.

His rental returned. He hopped out, held the door open, and his mother got out. She grinned at something he said, and then chattered the entire way to the door. He kissed her on the cheek, and she disappeared into the house. He strolled back to his car as if he were in a trance.

Patrick's head hung. "I can't believe she's gone. I didn't have enough time."

James fast-forwarded, and I yelled, "Stop! That car that just pulled up. Whose is it?"

"Mine. I pulled in front to ask Helen to open the garage so I could park the car."

We watched James walk to the front door and then go back to the car. It drove out of sight toward the garage.

I rubbed my temple. "It's too bad we don't have pictures of the driveway and garage areas."

"Of course we do." James brought his chair to the upright position.

The three of us turned in unison. Patrick said, "Why didn't you tell us?"

"No one asked."

Patty put down her soda. "What do you mean? The police asked if we had footage from the pool area."

He sighed and rubbed his hands on his shorts. "The backyard is not the garage. They never asked about that."

Patrick groaned. "What you are saying is you knew there was a separate system for the garage, but you didn't think to tell anyone about it?"

James licked his lips. "When you put it that way, it doesn't sound good."

I said, "Before we go to bed, I want to see where this other system is."

James pressed fast forward again.

We viewed Patrick picking up his mother for dinner and then escorting her to the door afterward. His car pulled away. Two hours later, the light-deprived footage showed Patrick's car return. He stopped at the curb but didn't leave the car. He drove away.

Patrick pointed at the screen. "See. This proves I didn't get out of the car."

We didn't see anything for another hour. Patty said, "You can tell this is an exclusive neighborhood because there's no one on the road. We have cars drive by our house all the time."

Just then, a car passed driving very slowly. It was some type of a sport utility vehicle, and the color was anywhere from a midnight blue to straight black.

I asked, "What's that car doing? Does anyone recognize it?"

"It didn't stop. And do you know how many SUVs are on the road these days?" James interjected.

"Yes," Patrick said.

James's eyebrow rose.

"What? I sell cars. Forty-three percent of cars sold are SUVs. Of course, that's where we live. Not sure what it is in Phoenix."

Patty frowned. "If we can find out how many people there are in Phoenix, we can—"

James held up his hand. "Less scientific, please. You've been driving around the past few days. How many SUVs have you seen?"

Patty said, "A lot. And, the odd thing was I didn't notice many in silver or white. They were mostly dark colors. You would think with the sun, people would stick to light colors."

No one else passed by the house till the next morning. We filed out of the theater, and I said, "At Helen's reception on Saturday, we'll have to pay attention to the kind of cars people drive."

* * *

Patty and I scooted out the door into the garage; Patrick followed. Patty said, "It's a shame James couldn't join us."

"His boss wanted something, and, to be frank, after everything that's been going on, I could use a break from him." Patrick pulled out of the driveway and stopped. "Let's use the GPS, James gave me directions, but I'm not quite sure where the restaurant is."

He patted his pockets. "The address is on my phone. I think I left it upstairs on the counter."

Patty's phone rang. "It's the kids."

I opened the door. "You two talk to the kids. I'll run in and look for it."

Patrick yelled after me, "Try our bathroom."

James jumped as I ran back in the door. I waved to him as I took the stairs two at a time. The phone wasn't on the counter. I checked the dresser and the shorts Patrick had been wearing early in the day. I didn't find it.

I ran back down. "James, could you do me a favor and call Patrick's phone? Mine's in my purse in the car."

Far away strains of "Sweet Child of Mine" by Guns and Roses played. I followed the sound and recovered Patrick's phone.

I dashed into the living room. "Found it."

James asked, "Where was it?"

"In his seat, in the movie room. Bye."

CHAPTER 15

Merry

The air conditioning in my room at night was set at sixty-five, which made sleeping under blankets comfortable but made for a cold walk to the bathroom. I lay on one side, curled up under the covers. My phone was in my right hand as I spoke with Rob. "I miss you too. Have you seen Jenny? She texted me yesterday, but I haven't talked to her."

"I took Jenny and the Twilliger clan out to a new burger joint last night. They had an old whack-a-mole arcade game, and I figured the kids would go crazy for it. They played till our dinners arrived. Jenny's having dinner with Jacob's family tomorrow night. What's going on in Phoenix?"

I brought him up to speed.

"What's wrong with Patrick's brother?"

"I know. You can tell Patrick and James are brothers. Both of them haven't been exactly forthcoming. Patrick didn't tell them he came back to the house that night until they discovered it, and James has consistently fudged the truth. What part about 'don't lie to the police' do you think he doesn't understand? James assumes if you don't ask him a specific question, he doesn't need to expand his answer."

"Sounds like a lawyer. How is he going to tell the police about the other system?"

"We told him to let his attorney handle it. James was going to call him this morning."

"Are you going to copy the CD before they take it?"

"I did last night."

Rob cleared his throat. "I'm nervous about you staying in the same house with him."

I pulled the covers further over my head; it felt cozy like the forts I used to make when I was younger. "I'm not staying here on my own, and my door is locked."

"Do you think he did it?"

"I hope not. Especially for Patrick's sake. It's going to be crazy at the funeral tomorrow. The caterer is sending chairs and tables today to stage for the reception."

"Sounds like quite the shindig."

"It'll be a nice send-off for Helen. It will also be good to meet her friends so we'll both get a better sense of the person she was."

"Be careful. Oh, by the way, Andy and Ed had quite the party for your new neighbors the other night. They're fun."

I sighed. "I wish I could have been there. Love you."

"Love you back. I'll make sure Jenny's fine."

"I know you will." I pressed end.

My doorknob rattled, and then there was a soft rap. "Merry, you up?"

I ran to the door, unlocked it, and hurtled back to bed.

Patty wandered in. "Patrick's still asleep. Are you getting up?"

"Yes—"

"Doesn't look like it. And, what temperature is it in here?" She shivered, moved to the thermometer, and pressed the up arrow. Then, she grabbed the soft taupe throw from the chair, draped it over herself, and sat.

I plumped my pillows and placed them behind me. "Why are you up so early?"

"Couldn't sleep. What if James did kill Helen? Patrick likes him, and he's the only blood relative he has left, besides our kids."

"Some heavy thoughts."

"Plus, I'm trying to figure out how to get a copy of the disc before the police come and take it."

I pulled open the drawer to my bedside table and pulled out a disc.

Her mouth dropped. "When did you do that?"

"Last night, after everyone went to bed."

"James could have done it this morning."

I looked away from her, toward the window.

"You were afraid he might erase something. Why wouldn't he have done that before now?"

✳ ✳ ✳

The caterers arrived just past noon with extra tables, decorations, and chairs. The police came shortly after that. They retrieved the disc and pulled James into a closed-door session in Helen's office, which got a little loud. I couldn't make out what they were saying, so I ambled to the kitchen for a snack of blueberry yogurt.

James wandered in a few minutes later to get more coffee. He nodded and poured a cup. "The police are becoming a pain."

"What did they say?"

"They made me swear this was the only other security camera. They also told me not to leave town." He perched on a stool. "I'm getting tired of Phoenix."

✳ ✳ ✳

The next morning, I donned a black dress and shoes. I debated wearing hose and decided the Phoenix heat was a great reason to be more casual. I unlocked the door to my room and made my way to the kitchen just as Patrick walked in with bagels and a large container of coffee. He held them up. "I told Matilda to put out paper plates and cups this morning. That way, no one has to do dishes."

"Great idea. Those smell wonderful." I paused. "How are you doing?"

He put the food on the table and sank onto a chair. "Tired, sad, and somewhat bitter. I still can't believe she's dead."

"This has to be stressful."

"It's also bewildering. What am I going to do with all this?" He extended his arm around the room. "Patty and I live in Hopeful. Should I keep this place? Sell it?"

I opened the container and poured coffee for us both. "Just worry about getting through today."

Heels clicked on the tile floor leading to the dining room. Patty strode through, wearing a black skirt, white shell, and dark rose jacket. She kissed Patrick's cheek as she reached for the bag of bagels. She placed one with sesame seeds on a paper plate and sat.

I passed her the cream cheese. "What a lovely comb."

Patty's brown hair was upswept, held in place by a delicate clip of golden leaves dotted with seed pearls and diamonds. She touched it. "Thanks. James thought I might like it, so he retrieved it from her room. It was one of her favorites."

James strode into the room and grabbed a pumpernickel bagel.

"It's a shame your children weren't able to be here," I said.

"Their mother said Helen wasn't related to them, so there wasn't any point."

My mouth made a perfect circle. "Family can be more than just blood relations. Did your children know Helen?"

"They spent the odd few weeks here over the years. Not really since my father died."

"That's sad. I hope when I have grandchildren, they'll want to be with me." I sipped my coffee.

Patrick placed his cup on the table. "My kids were devastated when my father died, and I expect they'll be as upset when my mother goes. And, they were my adoptive parents, not blood relatives."

James shrugged. "Every family is different."

"Apparently." Patrick stood. "I'm going to get dressed."

"But you didn't have anything to eat yet," Patty sputtered.

"Not hungry." He stalked from the room.

James said, "I wasn't trying to offend."

Patty took his hand. "He knows that. It's going to be a stressful day."

"All I know is I can't wait to lose this suit. It seems silly to wear one in this heat."

I stood. "Anyone want anything else?"

They shook their heads. I threw the plates in the trash and found a plastic bag for the left-over bagels. The caterer arrived, and it seemed like people were everywhere in the house. Before long, the black limo arrived, and we climbed in.

"This is the first time I've ridden in a limo to a funeral." I smoothed my dress. "How many people are coming?"

"Last count? Nearly five hundred."

I sat back. "Wow."

The limo pulled up in front of the church, and we got out. James led the way, and Katie waved to us from the door. "They're just about to start." We followed her down the aisle to the first pew. The church seemed about to pop, with people standing on the sides and all along the back.

I slid in first, followed by Patty, Patrick, and James. Katie moved to sit behind us, but James motioned for her to sit in our pew. She flashed him a grateful smile and sat.

The closed coffin rested at the end of the aisle. A beautiful arrangement of pink roses, stephanotis, and white lilies draped it, and the church smelled heavenly. I nudged Patty. "The casket is beautiful."

She nodded.

Strains of Vivaldi's "Winter" began, and the crowd grew silent. Patrick paled, and tears streaked his face as Patty rubbed his back. The Priest strode to the podium, and the ceremony began.

Several of Helen's friends had asked to speak. The first told a tale about how Helen had raised money for a new homeless shelter, the next mentioned how Helen had befriended her when she first came to town, and the last told an amusing story about Helen trying to teach Frank to fish. Frank had hooked "the big one," and when he leaned forward with the net to pull the fish in, a wave hit the boat, and he fell into the water on top of the fish. The crowd laughed, breaking some of the tension.

It was a lovely tribute, and before long, we had formed a receiving line at the back of the church. Katie stood at the beginning, introducing the guests to Patrick, Patty, and James. Wanting to be helpful, I stationed myself to the right, handing direction cards to the mourners inviting them to join us at the house. The church emptied, and Katie said, "I better get to the house to make sure everything's in order."

Patrick nodded and headed back up the aisle to speak with the funeral director, Patty followed in his wake.

James said, "Can I hitch a ride with you, Katie?"

"Of course. But we have to leave now."

"I'll let them know," I said. They hurried to her car, and I turned back toward the nave. Patrick had his hand on the coffin, and Patty stood silent at his side. The funeral director left the priest and walked toward them, so I edged closer.

"What's next?" Patrick asked.

"We'll take her back to the mortuary, carefully move her to the other coffin, and she will be cremated. Her remains will be ready for you to pick up sometime tomorrow afternoon. I'll call you to arrange a convenient time." The funeral director held out his hand.

Patrick shook it. "Thanks for taking such good care of her." He placed his hand on the casket one last time, and then he and Patty joined me.

We slid into the air-conditioned limo. Patrick stared out the window as the driver pulled away from the curb. After a few moments, he said, "How on earth are all those people going to fit into that house?"

Patty and I laughed at the break in the tension. I said, "I guess we're going to find out."

Cars were parked on either side of the street stretched out for what looked like a good mile, and there was a line of people waiting to get in the front door. The chauffeur pulled into the driveway and let us out by the garage door.

We squeezed through the door into the house and wove our way through to the kitchen. The caterer looked like a general, inspecting trays and dispatching them through to the living room and out to the terrace. James was by the pool talking to guests. He had changed into a pair of madras shorts and a black polo. Patrick loosened his tie. "That looks like a good idea. I'll be back in a few minutes."

Patty asked the caterer, "Everything okay?"

She nodded and filled another tray. I snagged a miniature crab cake before it left the room and popped it in my mouth.

"Are you going to change? Or are you just going to stand there and peel off goodies before they go out the door?" Patty asked.

"Changing's too much trouble. Let's get wine."

We found a bar that wasn't crowded. "Two chardonnays," I said. I handed Patty a glass. As we made our way to the pool, Patty stopped and thanked people for coming.

Matilda, Louisa, and Phillippe sat at a table near the pool under an umbrella. Louisa stood. "Thank you for giving us the day off. It was a lovely funeral, and I'm sure Helen is smiling down on us from heaven."

"I appreciate how you, Matilda, and Phillippe have kept things running during such a trying time." Patty dipped her head and moved to greet the next group. We finally found two empty seats in the shade.

She sank onto one and said, "Thank heavens for the misters, it would be so hot without them."

I nodded. "How are you doing?"

"It's so strange to be at the funeral of someone I've never met, yet who could have been so important to our family." She shook her head. "Who was so important to my husband. And, who I wish I could have met."

I sipped chardonnay and watched a Rufous hummingbird frolic in and out of the spray. He darted behind me and stopped at a flower on the hibiscus hedge for a drink. I could just make out a couple seated on the other side of the greenery. "I didn't think we hung misters back there."

Patty asked, "Where?"

I pointed. "It must be hot."

"The acacia provides shade."

"Still."

"You said you were going to take care of it." The man's voice rose.

"I tried. She told me she was going to change her will," someone mumbled.

"Work started because you were so sure. You signed a contract."

"I'll get it somehow. Don't worry."

"You better." The man stood and stalked away.

My eyes widened. "Could you see who that was?"

"No." Patty shook her head. "But I think I know who the woman is."

Katie rounded the hedge, wiping her eyes. She stopped abruptly when she saw us staring at her. Then she relaxed her shoulders and approached.

Patty pointed to the open seat next to her. "Please sit, and I'll get you a drink. You've been working so hard."

Katie slid onto the seat, and Patty walked over to stand in line at the pool bar.

I said, "You have great organizational skills; I can't believe you arranged this in only a few days."

Katie smiled. "It's a good event. I think Helen would feel I honored her."

"I'm sure she would. Tell me about her work with the theater."

Patty handed Katie a glass and sat back down. "Please do. I love learning more about her life and the things she did."

Katie sipped her wine. "I met her at one of the plays I starred in. The cast and I were running lines, and she sat in the back of the theater. After it was over, she took me to lunch. We became fast friends after that."

"Patrick mentioned she held fundraisers here," Patty said.

"She was so generous. Whenever we needed equipment or even a more well-known star, she'd reach for her pocketbook, or hold a gala." Katie sighed, "She was a true patron of the arts."

"Who will you tap now?" I leaned toward her.

She gasped. "Helen was far more than an ATM. She was a funny, lovely, caring person."

"I know that. But her demise must have left a gap in your expectations."

An older gentleman with a distinctive white mustache leaned over her chair. "Katie, my dear, I'm so sorry. Helen is such a great loss to the community. And, what does this do to your plans for the theater's restoration?"

Patty held out her hand. "We haven't been introduced. I'm Patty Twilliger, Helen's son's wife."

One white eyebrow rose. "I thought James was divorced."

"It's a long story." Katie rose and took the gentleman's arm. "Come along Gerard, let's get inside where it's cooler, and I'll bring you up to date."

I crossed my legs. "Isn't that interesting?"

* * *

The next morning I slept till eight, shockingly late considering what time I had been getting up this week. *Yesterday was exhausting with all those people.*

There was a quiet knock at my door. Then the doorknob wiggled.

I padded across the floor and unlocked the door. Louisa balanced a tray with delicious smelling coffee and a newspaper. I extended my arm into the room, and she put the tray down on the dresser. "Would you like your curtains open?"

"Yes, please. This is lovely. Coffee in my room, the paper delivered, I might not go home."

"If this was winter, I could believe it. But since it's summer—wait till you feel the heat in August." She laughed. "Do you need anything else?"

"This is perfection."

As she shut the door, I poured myself coffee and swirled in cream. *I could get used to this.* I sat on the chair by the French doors, put my feet on the ottoman, and opened the paper. The headline screamed, "Swindler Drew March to be extradited to the U.S." My mug slipped, and coffee fell onto the paper, myself, and the ottoman. Cursing, I grabbed a towel from the bathroom and mitigated the damage.

I searched for my phone. *My purse.* I pulled it out. Dead. I took the plug from the suitcase and inserted it into the outlet—four messages from Rob. I pressed play on the first one. "Merry, Drew's extradition just came over the AP wire. Call me." The next three were more of the same. *Darn.* I turned off my phone's ringer during the service yesterday and didn't check it before I went to bed.

Patty raced in. "Did you see the paper?"

I held it up.

"Rob texted me. He said to tell you to turn on your phone."

I called him. "Sorry. No juice, again."

"I'm at Patty's."

"Hold on, she's here, let me put you on speaker." I pressed the button.

"Patty's mom called me," he said. "Jenny's locked herself in Cindy's room. She said she's never coming out. Snapchat has blown up with Drew memes, and some of her classmates are not being very nice about it. They're bringing up his last conviction."

I groaned. "I'll call her." I pressed her number. No answer.

I called Rob again. "Tell her to pick up the phone."

Three raps and he relayed the message. He came back on the line. "She turned it off. Call her now."

I pressed her number. She answered, her voice gruff as if she'd been crying, "Mom, I don't want to live here anymore. People are so mean."

"I'm getting the first flight back today."

"Don't."

"You don't want me to come home?"

"I want to come there. I don't want to be here. It's too hard." She sobbed. "If it weren't for Jacob, I'd never want to live here again. I'd go somewhere new—where—where people don't know us."

"Hold on a minute."

I pressed the phone to my chest. "Is it okay if Jenny comes here?"

"Of course."

I put the phone to my ear. "Okay, you're coming. Do you want me to come back and get you?"

She sighed. "Mom, I can get on a plane by myself."

"Put Rob on."

There was a creak. Rob murmured, "It'll be okay, sweetie."

Jenny said, "Here he is."

"What's going on?" Rob asked.

"Jenny's going to come here. I'll book the flight and text you the details. Would you please take her to the airport?"

"Do you want me to come with her?"

"You have to cover that trade show in town. As much as I'd love to see you, she can come on her own. I need to arrange flights, so I'm going to hang up. Love you; give her a hug for me."

"Already am. Love you too."

I pressed end.

"What's happening?" Patty asked.

I put up my hand, signaling for her to wait. My fingers flew over the phone as I checked flights and booked Jenny on one arriving later in the day.

CHAPTER 16

Patrick

I had just poured Cheerios into a bowl when my phone rang. "It's not fair," Cindy whined. "She was my grandmother, and now Jenny gets to see her house first? Why can't I come with her?"

"What are you talking about? Jenny's coming to Phoenix?"

"Don't you and Mom talk? Jenny's dad's extradition came through. They're bringing him to New York."

Merry and Patty walked into the dining room. I said, "Hold on, Cindy," and put the phone down. "It's Cindy. She wants to come with Jenny."

Patty took the phone. "Cindy, I'm not sure that's a good idea. Grandma said you've been such a help with the boys."

"They're at camp all day. And, Mr. Jenson said he'd help. He's going to take them to the minor league baseball game tonight."

"Put Mr. Jenson on the phone. Rob? Are you sure? Are my parents okay with it? Thanks. I owe you big time."

"I'll send you Jenny's confirmation email," Merry said.

Patty's head bent over her phone. After a few minutes, she smiled. "Success. I even got them seats next to each other. Let me just send this to Rob."

Matilda walked in. "What would you two like for breakfast?"

"Cereal's fine with me," Patty said.

"Me too." Merry grabbed bowls from the sideboard.

"Matilda, we're going to have two seventeen-year-olds joining us tonight. It would be great if you would make French toast for them tomorrow. Also, if you would let Louisa know to make up the bedroom with the twin beds, I'd appreciate it." Patty poured milk on the cereal.

* * *

Everyone wanted to pick up the girls at the airport, so Louisa volunteered the use of their minivan. James drove. "What's my niece like?"

"She's special." My smile was soft. "Of course I'm a doting father, so you'd expect me to say that, but she is. She dances, plays basketball, and keeps her grades up. And, she's the nicest, kindest girl you could meet."

"Sounds like a great kid. We're going to have to get your clan and mine together so they can get to know each other. Mine are pretty special too." He turned into the airport parking lot and parked. We hurried toward baggage claim.

Merry ran toward Jenny and hugged her. Patty wasn't too far behind with Cindy. I reached them, picked Cindy up, and twirled her. "I've missed you."

"Dad, you're embarrassing me."

James held out his hand to Cindy. "I'm your Uncle James."

I grabbed Jenny's bag and hugged her. "Welcome to Phoenix."

Jenny said, "I'm sorry about your mother."

"I was sorry to read about your dad."

Merry put her arm around Jenny as they strolled toward the van. Patty spoke softly with Cindy. I asked, "How was the flight?"

"Long," Jenny said, "and the coach seats are all squished together."

Cindy rolled her eyes. "Be careful, you'll hear all about her first-class trip to London."

Jenny poked her arm. "I'm not that bad."

"Yes, you are." Cindy jumped on the mat for the automatic doors. They opened, and a fiery blast of heat blew in. "Whoa."

We arrived at the car, and the girls climbed into the third row of seats. James popped the hatch and loaded the bags.

Cindy griped, "Air, please."

James started the car and put the air on high. He pressed the button to roll the windows down as well. "It's going to take a few moments."

Sweat trickled down my back. As soon as cool air exited the vents, I shut the windows.

Jenny quipped, "I'm not sure we brought enough clothes if it's going to be this hot."

The girls bent over their phones. Jenny groaned, and Merry turned, took Jenny's phone, and dropped it into her purse in one smooth motion. "You don't need to see any more. Why don't you enjoy the sights?"

They began a running commentary, with Cindy and Patty chiming in. I tuned the chatter out and focused on what Patty told me about Katie last night. *What type of money had she been counting on from Helen? And, why had Katie thought Helen had made changes to her will to benefit the theater?*

"That's the house?" Cindy's cry interrupted my reverie as James pulled into the driveway.

Patty and Merry exited the van, and then Jenny and Cindy piled out.

"Wow." Jenny's eyes widened.

James took the suitcases from the back, and I opened the door to the house. Cindy ran in. "Look at those beams. They're so big." She turned. "A pool. And, hot tub. I can't wait. Where are our rooms? I want to get changed and get into the pool."

"You and Jenny are going to be sharing a room and a bath upstairs."

"Let's go." Jenny charged up the stairs, bag in hand.

Patty called, "Last door on the right." She, Merry, James, and I sank onto the sofa.

Merry poured a glass of iced tea from the pitcher on the coffee table. "Thanks for letting them come; I think a change of scenery is what Jenny needed. Although I don't know if Matilda and Louisa are ready for so much energy in the house."

A few minutes later, the girls charged down the stairs, making it sound like thunder. They raced out onto the patio and jumped in the pool.

Merry ran out. "Sunscreen! I don't want anyone getting burned."

"It's late," Jenny said.

Matilda walked from the kitchen to the patio with a tray containing a small ice chest, a bowl full of chips, and dip. "I thought you might like sodas and snacks."

Jenny and Cindy exchanged a glance. "This is the best," Cindy cried out as she cannonballed into the pool.

* * *

Patty curled up against my shoulder the next morning. "Should we have Louisa clean the girls' room? I mean, I don't want them to get used to this. It's not the way we live."

"They've been to hotels before. We don't make them clean the room when we go on vacation."

She shrugged. "I guess not. What are we going to do with all this?"

"One day at a time."

Cindy shrieked. I leaped out of bed, ran to her room, banged on the door, and opened it. "What? Are you okay? What's wrong?" Patty raced in behind me.

Cindy and Jenny huddled together, pointing at the wall, fingers shaking. A lizard made its lazy way toward the window. I picked it up. "It's just a gecko. It won't hurt you. It must have climbed in when Louisa opened the room yesterday."

I carried the squirming gecko down the hall as Louisa passed me. "Fresh squeezed orange juice for the girls."

Patty elbowed me. "No way they're going to be spoiled—"

She peeled off into our room to get dressed, and I trotted down the steps to release the lizard by the pool. Merry sat at one of the tables under an umbrella, typing on her laptop. She looked up. "What do you have there?"

I put the little guy down. "A gecko. Scared the girls."

She laughed.

"What are you doing?"

"Work. All play means I don't get paid."

I started back into the house.

"The French toast will be ready in about thirty minutes, so you may want to give the girls a heads up."

"Will do." I ran up the steps and knocked on the girls' door. "Thirty minutes to French toast."

I moved on to our bedroom and sat down in front of the bathroom mirror. While I was shaving, Patty jumped up to sit on the counter next to me. "We need to find time to look at the DVD when James isn't around."

The razor made practiced strokes on my face. I stuck my tongue into my cheek to push out a dimple. "We could watch it with James there. He didn't kill Helen."

"Then why didn't he tell the police about the garage camera when they came to get the tapes for the other one. Something's fishy."

"I'm just getting to know him. I don't want him to think I don't trust him." I splashed my face with water and toweled it dry.

Patty kissed my cheek. "He doesn't need to know we watched—maybe you two should take the girls out today. I'm sure James wants to get to know Cindy better."

"I did read something about tubing on the Salt River through the Tonto National Forest." I paused and then frowned. "I'm still not happy about you and Merry watching the tape. It feels wrong."

Patty glanced at her phone. "Oops. Need to get moving."

We walked down the stairs and into the dining room.

✳ ✳ ✳

Shortly before ten, James and I loaded the car. Matilda had given us two coolers, one with water and sodas, the other filled with a picnic and snacks. She had given us a stern admonishment to wear t-shirts over our bathing suits and to bring hats. I drove to the parking area, where we selected an inner-tube for each of us and smaller ones for the coolers.

Cindy said, "Hurry up. It's hot out here."

I draped my beach towel over the inner-tube, to use it as a sling for my body. James smiled. "It looks like you've done this before." He and the girls followed suit.

Soon the river had us meandering along, viewing scrub and the occasional coyote on the banks.

James paddled nearer my float. "What are Merry and Patty up to today?"

"I think they mentioned doing some shopping." I averted my eyes and felt my face warm from the lie.

CHAPTER 17

Merry

"I thought they would never leave." I popped the DVD into the player, walked to the door of the theater, and locked it.

"Why did you lock the door?"

"Just being careful."

"You don't think they had anything to do with this?" Patty tossed popcorn in her mouth, some of it dribbled onto the floor.

"They inherited too, don't forget." I sat next to Patty. "I'm going to go fast on this. Hopefully, we'll see something." I started the afternoon of Patrick's arrival. That went by quickly since most of the action that day happened in front of the house. Later that night, a light gray sedan pulled into the drive, and then the garage door opened.

"That's James's rental. It must have been when he arrived." Patty pointed at the screen.

I checked the time on the machine, looked at my notes, and nodded. "The time checks with the other tape. He said he went to the front first to let Helen know he was there and to have her open the garage door."

The next morning, Matilda's car pulled into the driveway at six and parked on the side. She walked in through the door by the garage. I said, "Huh. I wonder why we didn't see her car the day before."

"Wait. I remember Patrick telling me that was the employees' day off." A short while later, James's car pulled out. "That must be when James went to meet Patrick for breakfast."

Phillipe and Louisa arrived next. He parked, she went in the side door, and Phillipe continued around the back out of sight of the cameras. James came and went throughout the day, and Helen left in her light blue Mercedes. Later on, James's car exited with Helen in the passenger seat. I said, "That must have been when they were meeting Patrick for dinner."

An hour later, James's car careened into the driveway. He leaped out and stalked to the door. Patty sat back in her chair. "He looks mad."

"If you'd just found out someone was going to get more of the share of the inheritance you'd been counting on, you'd be mad too."

About three hours later, James hopped back in his car and backed out. Patty's eyes widened. "He didn't say he left the house that night."

"Nope."

A few minutes later, a dark SUV drove slowly past the driveway and out of the frame. I checked my notes. "I think we saw that car go past the front of the house too." I pulled the other DVD from my purse. Let's queue this one up again for roughly the same time." I pointed. "There. Is that the same car?"

"It looks like it. Who do we know with a dark SUV?" Patty frowned. "I think I saw several in the funeral home parking lot, but they could have belonged to anyone."

I popped the other DVD back in the player. Two hours later, a cab pulled up. James exited, looking unsteady. He stumbled and just before the door tripped and crashed into it. "He looks drunk."

Patty nodded. "Plus, where's his car?"

Like clockwork, Matilda arrived with the sun at six, and then Louisa and Phillipe at eight. By nine-thirty, lights from police cars swirled in the driveway.

I pressed stop. "Now, we have three questions we need answered. Why did James not want us to see this, and where did he go? And, does Helen know anyone who drives a dark-colored SUV?"

"Which one should we tackle first?"

"Let's have lunch and talk about it."

"We had French toast for breakfast!"

"And your point is?"

Patty hung her head. "I could eat. Let's see what Matilda has on tap."

I unlocked the door, and we ventured toward the kitchen. I said, "Follow my lead."

Patty nodded.

Just before we stepped into the kitchen, I said loudly, "I think SUV's are so durable. I may look into getting one when we get back."

Patty started to giggle, and I glared at her. She pushed the door open and said, "They are nice. I wouldn't mind one myself."

Matilda looked up. "They're okay, but they guzzle so much gas."

"It's too bad I can't ask someone I trust about its performance and which brand to get." I leaned against the kitchen counter.

Matilda put down the spoon she was using to mix tuna salad. "I don't know if I trust her, but Katie has a black Mercedes SUV."

*   *   *

"This theater is so pretty. I love the painted ceiling and gold embellishments, though the peeling paint makes me nervous. I'd be constantly thinking paint chips were landing in my hair." Patty leaned on the railing leading to the seats to get a better view. It creaked, and she jumped backward.

I wiggled the rail. "This could stand to be repaired."

Patty pointed to a large sign on the far side of the aisle. "Restoration coming soon. Donate!" It listed a crowdfunding site. "Huh. I wonder how the fundraising is going."

126

"From what that guy said to Katie, she was relying on getting money from Helen." My eye trailed up the ornate and somewhat rickety-looking staircase. "It's going to take quite a bit of restoration."

Patty rubbed the fabric on the seats. "From my experience as a designer, these types of fabrics don't come cheap."

Katie ran up the aisle. "Sorry to keep you waiting, we were conducting the first run through in the back."

"We drove by and decided to stop. It's a lovely theater. Too bad it's been allowed to deteriorate," I said.

"It'll come back. It may take a while, but we'll raise the funds." Her chin jutted.

"I have no doubt. What's your battle plan?"

"I have an hour break; let's go to the coffee shop next door, and I'll tell you all about it."

She led the way, and Patty and I followed. Katie ordered an Americano and a spinach salad; Patty and I chose lattes and a peanut butter cookie to split.

We sat at one of those wrought-iron bistro tables that look cute but leave you wanting more surface area. Juggling three big coffee cups, a salad bowl, and the plate for our cookie, we made it work.

"I want to thank you again for giving Helen such a terrific send-off. You thought of everything, and I don't know what we would have done without you." Patty sipped coffee.

Katie beamed. "It was a pleasure to honor Helen, and I'm so glad you felt it went well."

"It was good to meet all of Helen's friends. Such interesting stories." I snapped a piece of cookie off and dipped it in my latte.

"She was well-loved by the community and was doing important work. Especially for the theater."

Patty and I held our coffees so Katie could put a flipbook on the table. The first page showed the theater's current ceiling. The second an artist's rendering of what it could look like.

Patty gasped. "That's lovely. Look at the brush strokes. And, the cherubs."

She then showed us the before and after of the grand staircase. The repaired wood gleamed. "Isn't it beautiful?"

"It is. But this kind of restoration isn't cheap."

"Our plan is to do it a little at a time. We'd start with safety issues and then work our way up to the larger jobs." She flipped the pages to a schedule in the back. It was a ten-year plan costing a total of twenty million dollars.

I gasped. "That's a lot of money. How much have you raised so far?"

"Roughly a hundred thousand."

Mid-sip, Patty coughed. "You have a way to go."

Katie put her fork on the table. "The theater's all I know. I grew up in Central City."

"I don't know where that is."

"Downtown Phoenix and the airport area. It's pretty seedy now, but there used to be all these cool old buildings. They've put up high rises and office towers, but they forgot there were still people living there. All that steel is so impersonal." She shivered. "I studied hard and got scholarships. And I networked so that every summer, I would have an internship somewhere in town. That's how I got to know all the important people—the ones with influence, with money.

"I studied them and my roommates in college. They led such different lives. I was a scholarship student, had to work for spending money. But I was a theater major. I was trained to be someone else, to mimic others. So, I did." She pointed at her clothes. "Designer clothes for almost nothing by shopping at consignment stores. It made me look well off. I looked like I knew the secret handshake and belonged.

"My plan all along was to make a difference. Some actors want to go to California. Be in the movies. Not me. I love live theater and want to do it here. Part of it is giving back; the other part is to reinvent myself in the town where I grew up. What better way to do that than to restore part of our heritage? And, if that gives me a place to showcase my talents, even better." She laughed. "More information than you probably wanted."

Patty leaned forward. "I can tell it's from your heart."

"It definitely is. Have you and Patrick decided if you're keeping the house?"

"Right now, we're taking things one day at a time."

She handed me the flipbook. "Keep it. If you decide to stay, there's no better way to get involved than to invest in your community."

We stood and placed our plates and cups in the proper receptacles. "Thanks again for your hard work, and I'll talk to Patrick." Patty held up the book.

Just as Katie started to walk back to the theater, I said, "Katie, I almost forgot."

She turned.

"Were you driving near Helen's house the night she died?"

Her face paled.

"Security cameras. We saw your car."

"Helen was mad at me for asking Patrick to prove who he was, and we argued. I drove by to see if her light was still on so I could talk to her. Make her understand I didn't have an ulterior motive. I was just trying to protect her. Her light was off, so I went home." Katie's eyes grew moist. "I wish now I had stopped."

Katie turned and walked back to the theater, and Patty and I strolled to the car. I slid in the passenger seat. "I think I'm starting to like her."

"Me too."

"But, her story gives her an even better motive to kill Helen. And, she just admitted she was in the vicinity."

✳ ✳ ✳

After dinner, the girls adjourned to the pool house for a video game tournament, Patty and I sat in the living room, a cordial glass of Bailey's in hand, and Patrick flipped TV channels in search of something interesting to watch.

James wandered through. "Do you think the girls saw enough of us today, or should we see if they're up for some competition?"

Patty said, "Sit for a minute, James. The girls can wait."

"What's up?" He pulled a can of soda from the fridge and sat.

"Were you here all night, the night Helen was killed?"

Patrick put down the remote. "What are you talking about?"

"I told you. I was playing games out in the pool house. Then I spoke with Helen later." James sipped his cola.

"So, you never left the house?"

He put the can down. "What is it you think I did?"

"Nothing. You didn't do anything," Patrick protested.

I leaned forward. "James, we saw you leave around midnight. You didn't get home till past two."

"The garage tape. You duplicated it before the police got it." He stared at the coffee table.

I said, "Guilty. And, I don't think we're the only ones who will be asking you questions."

He stood, then paced. "It wasn't anything. As I said, I swam laps, realized the error of my ways, apologized to Helen, and played games in the cabana. It's boring playing alone, so I decided to treat myself to a nightcap with other like-minded adults. So I left."

I sat back on the sofa. "Where did you go?"

"A little dive bar named 'Seedy's' about a mile and a half down the road. You know the kind, cement-block building, small windows, and residual smoke from when it used to be legal. I came back here around three."

Patrick groaned. "What are the police going to think? First, you didn't tell them about the front camera, then they find out about the garage security, and now you've left the house. By the time you're done, they won't believe a word out of your mouth. Come with me." He stood.

James squirmed. "To play video games?"

"To call your lawyer. Into the den. Now." James stood and preceded Patrick into the den. Patrick shut the door. After ten minutes, Patrick eased out the door and plopped next to Patty on the sofa. "His lawyer berated him for ten minutes. He wants a copy of the DVD we have. I think James is going to be in there a while." Patrick put his arm around Patty. "A little heads-up would have been appreciated."

I leaned forward. "Now, let's tell you about Katie."

CHAPTER 18

Merry

Jenny knocked on my door, and when I answered, she shot past me and catapulted into bed. I climbed in next to her, and she put her ice-cold feet on mine. I yelped. "Don't you have slippers?"

"You pack slippers to go to a place where the average temperature is in the hundreds?"

I sighed. "To what do I owe the unexpectedly early pleasure of your company?"

"What's going to happen to Dad?" She frowned.

I touched her face. "I'm not sure. He's going to be brought to New York next Friday, and after that, he'll likely be in jail till his trial."

"He'll be in jail?" She scooched closer and lay her head on my arm.

"He was one step ahead of the FBI when he went to Brunei. I'm sure they'll classify him as a flight risk. Arianna, too, perhaps. You need to prepare yourself that this is going to go on for a while."

She groaned. "I wish this was over."

"You and me both." I twirled her long blonde hair around my finger. "What do you want to do today?"

"Can we be lazy? I'd like to lay by the pool and just chill."

"I have to do some work, but after I'm done, I'll join you."

* * *

Patty and Cindy were already downstairs by the time Jenny and I got out of bed. Cindy said, "Mom and I were talking about going shopping today. Want to go?"

Jenny gave me an uncertain look.

"Can she take a raincheck?" I asked. "We're just going to chill by the pool."

"Sounds like fun," Patty buttered an English muffin. "We'll join you when we get back. Patrick and James have inheritance stuff going on, so they'll be gone most of the day too."

Matilda walked in with a large stack of blueberry pancakes. "Who wants one?"

Jenny held out her plate. "This is great. Just like a five-star resort. Thanks, Ms. Matilda."

Cindy took two, smeared them with butter and syrup, and ate a forkful. She sighed, "The best."

Matilda beamed as she walked back into the kitchen. I refilled my coffee mug and stood. "The sooner I get started on my to-do pile, the sooner I can play by the pool."

I placed my laptop on Helen's desk and plugged it in. It was such a pretty room, and the chair seemed to fit my height exactly. *Maybe I should redo my office at home.*

My phone rang. "Hi, Cheryl. How's everything back at the office?"

She gave me an update and walked me through the emails that required my attention. I hung up and dove in. One of my clients was disputing details of her bill. I pulled up a copy and realized it would be easier if I wrote down the figures, versus switching back and forth to the spreadsheet on my computer. I pulled open the drawer to Helen's desk and looked for a pen and a piece of paper. As neat as the office was, the desk drawer was a different story. I found a pen but had to check two other drawers to find paper. A stack of blank pages was wedged under a red binder. When I yanked one of the pieces, the binder flew out and hit the floor.

Nice work, Merry. I sighed as I bent to pick it up. It was open to pages that looked like household accounts for the previous month. The headers were groceries, cleaning supplies, landscaping, entertainment, charities, etc. Someone had circled several of the numbers with a red pen and had inserted question marks near the entries. I pulled it closer. *Two thousand for groceries for the month?* I gasped. *Who could spend that much, especially when the person lived alone?* I paged back to the preceding month. Close to the same amount and nearly identical for the one before that. Maybe Helen entertained all the time? Katie said she held fundraisers. But wouldn't those come under entertainment or charities? I was sure Helen would have wanted to write them off on her taxes.

I closed the book and put it back in the drawer. I'd have to figure out a way to get to the bottom of this, but for now, I needed to help my client with her bill. Pen in hand, I puzzled on it until I realized the insurance company mistakenly charged her for more square feet in the building than were actually there. I sent off a note to the insurer about the discrepancy.

My stomach growled, and I checked the time. Nearly one, no wonder I was hungry. I stretched and went in search of sustenance. Jenny was lying in the shade by the pool, reading a book. I walked out onto the patio. "Is it any good?"

She nodded.

"Have you had lunch?"

Jenny swung her legs to the side of the chaise lounge. "Not yet. I was waiting for you. Can we have it out here?"

"As long as it's in the shade. Do you want anything in particular?"

"Surprise me." She reopened her book.

I wandered into the kitchen. Matilda had her head bent over a zucchini, scraping the seeds. She said, "I thought we'd have stuffed zucchini for a vegetable tonight. I got freshly ground chorizo at the store."

"Sounds yummy." I sat on a stool by the island. "I know you're busy prepping for dinner. If you don't mind, I'll make Jenny and myself a sandwich."

She pointed with her knife toward the refrigerator. "There are assorted ones in there, help yourself. I also made a fresh fruit salad and blackberry iced tea."

I put a few sandwiches on a plate, dished out the fruit, and poured two glasses of tea. "Tray?"

Matilda nodded to the side of the refrigerator. "Right there."

"We keep adding to the number of people staying at the house, and nothing seems to bother you." I loaded the lunch goodies on the tray.

"Back when the Mr. was alive, I served quite a few people. Since then, an occasional event, but other than that, Helen kept pretty quiet. She didn't eat much either, some soup, nothing too elaborate. It's been nice to have a full house again. I like cooking for a crowd."

"You do it so well." I lifted the tray and started for the door.

"There are fresh-baked chocolate chip cookies in the jar if you feel like a snack later." She held the door for me.

I put the tray on the table. If Helen was just having soup, what on earth was she spending the money on?

Patty and Cindy returned around three, weighed down by shopping bags. They brought their prizes to the pool, where Jenny and I were relaxing. I put down my book. "Looks like there's probably not a lot left in the stores."

"Don't be silly. Two or three things might still be there. We got the boys a souvenir since they're stuck at home, and we bought ourselves some stuff since we've been here longer than I anticipated." She plopped a bag on top of my legs, and Cindy dropped a bag on top of Jenny.

I sat up. "What's this?"

"A surprise, since you were kind enough to brave Phoenix in the summer."

"You didn't have to do that." I opened the bag. It contained white slacks and two colorful short sleeve shirts. "Nice!"

Jenny's bag contained a new aqua and rose bikini and matching cover-up. "This is pretty! Thanks." She threw her arms around Cindy and Patty and hugged them.

They gathered their remaining bags. "We'll be back down in a few. Do you want us to drop your bags in your room?"

I said, "Please." They took them and left.

"That was a nice surprise."

"It was. Do you think we should let them in on the chocolate chip cookie information?"

"At the very least." Jenny laughed.

A few minutes later, Patty and Cindy claimed the lounge chairs next to us. Patty sighed. "This is the life."

Cindy turned to Jenny. "Up for laps?"

"You're on."

"Cindy and I stopped by the funeral home on the way back from shopping to pick up Helen's remains. I put her on the mantle in the great room."

"I'm sure Patrick will appreciate that. There's so much going on."

I shut my eyes, and the steady rhythm of feet and hands propelling the girls through water lulled me to sleep. I jerked awake when Matilda dropped ice cubes in my glass and refilled the ice tea.

She said, "I didn't mean to wake you. It's so hot out I thought you might want more."

"I appreciate it." I laughed. "You must have been tiptoeing."

She handed a glass of tea to Patty and said, "Do you know what Cindy wants?"

"I'll ask her when she gets out."

Matilda put a dish of fruit on the table between us and then strode back into the kitchen.

I pulled my sunglasses down my nose and peered over them at Patty. "Did you hear her come out?"

"Nope."

"Creepy. By the way, how much do you and Patrick pay for groceries a month?"

"I don't even like to think about it. We try to keep our costs below fourteen hundred a month. Why?"

My mouth dropped. "That much?"

"We do have six people in the family, and four of them are boys. I guess when there are only two of you, that must seem like a lot." She nibbled on a grape.

"It may interest you to know Helen was paying over two thousand a month for hers." I popped a grape in my mouth.

* * *

We met downstairs at six for cocktails. Matilda laid out a cheese plate, mini tacos, and shrimp with cocktail sauce. Jenny and Cindy loaded their plates. I took a glass of red wine from James and said to Jenny, "Don't forget, we're also eating dinner." I was treated to the expected eye roll.

Helen's ashes were in a white-marble square container. It featured a pink rose on the top and had delicate rose veining in the marble. "This is lovely."

Patrick stood and raised his wine glass. "To Helen."

"To Helen, may she rest in peace," James echoed as Patty and I lifted our glasses and the girls their lemonade.

Patty sat. "It's been a busy day. What happened at the lawyers?"

"We signed our lives away." Patrick held his right hand out to Patty. "So many documents, my hand may never be the same again."

She kissed his hand. "Poor baby. What's the plan?"

James handed Patrick a martini. "Some of the money we can access right away. The estate can pay for Helen's funeral, the party, etc. Some of it we won't get until later. The lawyer is waiting to start the process of transferring the house and Mercedes to Patrick until the twelve days are up."

"Mercedes?" Cindy sat next to Patrick. "We get the Mercedes? The light blue convertible? I'd look great in that car."

"Cindy, my mother died. Let's not dance on her grave." Patrick frowned.

Her eyes welled. "I'm sorry, Dad."

"It's okay." He hugged her. "Besides, your first car needs to be big and built like a tank. I don't want my little girl to get hurt."

"Her first car was a Lamborghini." Cindy pointed at Jenny.

"Yeah, but I only got to drive it once." Jenny dipped a shrimp in cocktail sauce.

"What else did he have to say?"

"He's going to pay the money to Katie, Matilda, Louisa, and Phillipe. Since the bulk of the estate is going to Patrick and me, we can cover any taxes that might be owed. He said he might be able to get the money to them as early as next week," James said.

Matilda walked into the living room with more ice. "Next week?"

"Don't quote us on that, but he thought he might be able to."

"I'd rather have Helen, but I'm not going to lie. That money will be welcome. Dinner in fifteen minutes." She walked out the door.

My eyebrow rose. "I wonder what she needs the money for."

James elbowed me. "Everyone needs money."

CHAPTER 19

Patrick

Patty turned toward me, lying on her side, head propped on one arm. "You're going to need to talk to her about it. You can't slough it off on James; this is our house."

I groaned. "It happened before I was here. Can't we just ignore it?"

"Helen must have circled those items in red. Maybe she talked to Matilda about it. Maybe that's the reason she's dead."

"You don't think Matilda killed Helen? She's been feeding us for the past week, and Helen for umpteen years before that. If Helen was poisoned, I could see it. But she wasn't. Someone smothered her."

"She knew everyone would suspect her if it were poison. This way, it could be anyone, you, James, Katie, anyone."

My eyebrow rose. "Me?"

She shifted closer and draped my arm across her shoulders. "Never you. But she seems smart. And, so quiet. You barely know she's moving around. I think the police should be looking at her."

"I'll talk to her."

"Good." Patty kissed my nose, and her stomach growled.

"Let's get up; I think you need food."

"Hard as that is to believe." Patty slid out of bed and poured the coffee Louisa had dropped off earlier. "Want some?"

I stood. "You shower first. I'll get my own coffee."

She traipsed into the bathroom. I picked up a mug and began to fill it. The paper's headline caught my eye. "Police Stymied in Socialite

Helen McGregor Murder Case." I put the carafe on the table and sank onto the chair. The article rehashed how she was found and mentioned the police were questioning suspects. The implication from the article was they weren't moving fast enough.

The shower stopped. I handed the paper to Patty as we changed places. Her eyes widened at the headline.

* * *

Later that morning, I asked Matilda to meet me in Helen's office. I sat in Helen's chair and felt it wobble slightly. *If we keep the house, I'm going to need a bigger chair.* I extended my arm for her to sit in one of the facing chairs. "Matilda, I was cleaning out some of the things in Helen's desk, and I found this binder."

Her face paled.

I opened to the page Merry had found, flipped the book toward Matilda, and pointed to the totals. "As a father of four and a member of a six-person household, it's difficult for me to understand how Helen could be spending over two thousand on groceries per month."

"You should see what we've spent over the last week." She stood.

"Matilda, I own this house now, and you work for me."

"If you haven't been happy with my performance—"

"I've been pleased with how you've coped, and we all agree your food is wonderful. I just need to know what happened. Please sit."

She did. "It's not just Helen who ate here. She provided meals for me, Louisa, and Phillipe. And, she occasionally invited guests for dinner or lunch. Like Katie. Katie was a frequent guest."

I cleared my throat. "I understand that. And I understand Helen had a much higher standard of living than my family does. But it still doesn't add up."

"There's a foster care facility here in town. They don't have a lot, and Helen was giving them food every month. She had me take it out of the grocery account." Her hands clenched and unclenched the arms of her chair.

"Why wouldn't she have noted it as a charitable deduction? She deducted other things."

Matilda shifted in her seat. "I asked her about that. She said it was atonement. I never understood, but now that you're here, maybe I do. She had me drive the groceries in my car. I don't think she wanted to be identified as the benefactor. Maybe she didn't want people to know she had a child. I certainly didn't."

I sat back in the chair, mind swirling. Atonement? Had she been giving food to make up for turning her back on me?

"Will there be anything else?" Matilda stood.

I shook my head.

Patty edged through the door a minute after Matilda left and shut it behind her. "What happened?"

I told her.

"If that's true, why was Helen so open with everyone when you showed up? She introduced you as her son. You said she even seemed proud to acknowledge you."

I traced the notations Helen had made in the binder. "And, if she knew where the money was going, why did she circle these?"

"Did Matilda give you the name of the facility?"

"She didn't. And I don't want to ask her about it now. She was upset enough."

"How many foster care facilities can there be in Phoenix?"

I googled it. "A quick search gives me around fifty. That's a lot, but it's not a massive amount."

Merry rapped on the door and stuck her head in. "What happened?"

Patty waved her in, and Merry sat in the seat Matilda had vacated. I brought her up to speed. Merry asked, "Are we going to start calling them?"

I tapped the pen on the desk. "Why don't we start with the one from which I was adopted. If she was 'atoning,' that may have been the one she picked."

"Name?" Patty picked up her phone.

"Arms Circled Foster Care."

"Not finding it. It might not still be around."

"Who regulates foster care in Phoenix?" Merry asked.

I checked my phone. "Arizona Department of Child Safety."

"Do they have a licensing area?"

I nodded.

"Maybe start with them. They would know if it continued under a new name." Merry's phone buzzed. "Oops. Got to go." She left, phone pressed to her ear.

"I'll call." I pressed the phone number. "Hi. I was adopted from one of your facilities in the late 70s. I can't seem to find the name and wondered if they had gone out of business, or rebranded—Arms Circled Foster Care."

The clerk said, "Hold on—uh-huh. They changed their name in the nineties to Havenly."

"Heavenly?"

"H-a-v-e-n-l-y," he spelled it.

"Thanks for your help." I pressed end.

My eyes met Patty's. "They changed their name in the '90s. The new name is Havenly Foster Care."

She did a quick search. "Here it is. Visit or phone?"

"Visit."

* * *

We left Cindy and Jenny by the pool, and Merry working in the study and drove north. Patty said, "What's the plan?"

"What do you mean?"

"Our approach. What are we going to say?"

"We're going to tell them the truth. That I was adopted from their facility, and that I heard my birth mother was giving them food donations through Matilda."

Patty chewed on a fingernail.

"What's bothering you?"

"If what Matilda said is true, then their relationship was with her and not Helen."

My eyebrow rose.

"What if they call Matilda after we leave?"

"Why would that be a problem?"

"She'll feel we were checking up on her."

"We are."

Patty gave an exaggerated sigh. "If you investigated something I said, I wouldn't like it. And, if I worked for that person, it would make me wonder if this was going to become a habit. That might make me seek alternative employment."

"You're right. If we decide to keep this place, we'll need someone to run it. And, I don't have the first idea how to find someone."

"I agree we should tell the foster facility who we are. As for the rest of it, let's just see what kind of information we can get."

"That's your plan?"

She pointed. "It's this left; you'll have to make a quick turn."

I put on my blinker, slowed, and swerved into the parking lot. The person behind me honked. I waved and mouthed sorry. After parking, I turned to Patty. "Maybe we should think about this."

"Nope. Let's go." She hopped out of the car.

I got out more slowly and studied the bland dark-brown storefront. It didn't look familiar to me, and that bothered me for some reason. I was just a few days old the last time I'd been here; silly to think I'd remember it, but I wished I could. It seemed like such a momentous occasion. My adoptive parents must have stood in this same spot, happy their dreams for a child were about to be fulfilled.

Patty took my arm. "Ready?"

I nodded as we walked up the few steps and into the building. As I opened the door, my heart rate increased tenfold, my hands became clammy, and I worried about being able to speak.

The office was a beehive of activity. We approached the front desk, and I cleared my throat, testing it. "We'd like to see the manager, please."

The harried person glanced up. "Do you have an appointment?"

"No. I didn't know I'd need one. You see I came through here, forty-one years ago—"

"We don't divulge names of birth parents. There's a process you need to go through with the state." He pointed to a wall full of forms. "Fill out that one; the one in the middle, and send it to them. If your birth parents want to be contacted, they'll let you know."

"I already know who my birth parents are—" I was speaking to the top of his head as he had already turned back to his pile of paperwork. "Excuse me."

An older woman of about sixty approached the desk. "Is there a problem? How can I help?"

The clerk said, "They wanted to speak with you, but they don't have an appointment. I told them to fill out the form."

"Are you looking for your birth parents?"

I groaned. "I was just telling him I already know who my birth parents are."

"Then, why are you here?"

A few people who had been busy filling out forms and other workers in the office were now staring our way. I asked, "Is there a place that's more private?"

"Of course. This way." She led us to her office. "I'm afraid I only have a few minutes. We're trying to place children from the border crossings."

Patty and I sat. Patty said, "My husband recently found his birth mother. Unfortunately, she died soon after they were reunited."

"How sad." She turned to me, "I'm sorry for your loss. How can I help?"

I leaned forward. "We wanted to know if someone named Matilda was bringing you food every month."

"We don't accept food donations. We have nowhere to keep it. We accept diapers, personal hygiene items, clothing, and gift cards or cash for our foster children and families."

"So, you don't know a Matilda?"

She shook her head and stood. "Was there anything else?"

Patty and I walked back to the car, and I opened the door for her. "Matilda lied."

"We don't know that. Maybe she was taking them somewhere else. Maybe other facilities accept food."

I shut the door and walked to the other side of the car. *She lied right to my face.*

Patty was on her phone when I dropped into my seat.

"Uh-huh. You don't take food?" She hung up.

"You're calling the other facilities?"

"May as well."

My hands shook as I started the car, and I felt like I might be sick to my stomach. I gulped some water, which helped. *Such a nondescript place to have had such a significant impact on my life.*

* * *

Merry, Jenny, and Cindy were by the pool when we returned. Patty ran up the stairs to change, and I walked out to the patio.

Cindy said, "Dad, get your suit on. We want to put the net up for volleyball."

"In a minute."

Merry looked up from her book. I gestured toward the door with my eyes. She stood, donned her cover-up, and said, "Anyone want anything more to drink?"

Cindy and Jenny chimed in unison, "Water."

I walked back inside, and Merry followed. "Well?"

"In Helen's office." We walked down the corridor, and I shut the door behind her. "The foster care facility we visited doesn't accept food donations. On the way home, Patty called most of the other ones we found, none of them take food either."

"Hmm. So, Matilda lied."

"It would appear so."

The doorbell rang, and I walked out of the office and opened the door. Lieutenant Muniz and Detective Schwartz stood on the path. I said, "What is it now?"

"Is James McGregor here?"

"I think so. Last I heard he was planning on working in the library."

I walked the police to that door and knocked. James called out, "Come in."

The police opened the door. "James McGregor, you are under arrest for the murder of Helen McGregor. You have the right to remain silent and refuse to answer questions—"

The Miranda warning droned on, and I couldn't believe it—they were arresting James. I pulled out my phone and pressed the number for his attorney.

CHAPTER 20

Merry

As Patty traipsed down the stairs, James was being led away in handcuffs. Her mouth dropped, and she shouted, "James!" He turned and shrugged just before the door shut. She ran to Patrick. "What happened?"

"They arrested James."

"I could see that. Why?"

I said, "Probably because the press got on the police for dragging their heels. At least I hope that's what happened."

"Or they found new evidence." Patty turned to Patrick. "Did you call his lawyer?"

"While they were reading him his rights."

"He knows to keep his mouth shut." I walked into the living room and sat on the sofa.

Patty paced. "We have to do something. We can't just sit here."

"I agree. I think we should visit the police and tell them what we've uncovered."

"Are you going to tell them we took a copy of the camera DVDs?" Patty sat next to Patrick.

"We need to be upfront with them. It's the only way they're going to tell us what they know." I slipped my sandals on my feet.

"Our house. We're within our rights." Patrick pulled Patty close, "I've seen enough of the inside of the police station. Do you mind if I stay here?"

"Merry and I can handle it."

* * *

Patty and I slipped into Helen's Mercedes—the interior was a plush white leather, unmarked by kids, with a mahogany dashboard. There was a push-button to retract the convertible top. "Want the top down?"

I adjusted the air, so it blew on my face. "Are you kidding me?"

"You're no fun."

"This car fits you."

"It does. Who knows, I may drive it back."

I laughed. "I called the station to let them know we're coming."

"What are we going to tell them?" Patty flipped on the signal.

"Everything." I played with the radio, found a station with nineties tunes and Patty and I sang along. She groused, "This would be far more fun with the top down. Kind of a *Thelma and Louise* thing."

My eyebrow rose. "You do remember they die at the end."

"At least they had fun before they went." Patty pulled into a visitor's spot in the parking lot. "Let's go." We scurried across the parking lot and opened the door to the station. It seemed only slightly cooler. Wiping her forehead, Patty complained, "Do they even have the air on?"

"Your public tax dollars at work." I approached the front desk. "Meredith March and Patty Twilliger to see either Detective Schwartz or Lieutenant Muniz."

The sergeant led us back to Lieutenant Muniz's office. It had a chalkboard in one corner with various assignments written on it. His metal desk was large, with a scratched top, and the office chair was wooden and looked sturdy. He rose. "Ladies, please have a seat. What can I do for you?"

I extended my hand, and he shook it. "I'm Meredith March, a friend of Patty and Patrick's." I sat on one of the two hard straight-backed wooden chairs facing his desk.

Patty lowered herself onto the other one. "Thanks for seeing us, Lieutenant. We have information that may be useful."

He leaned back in his chair, and it squealed. "To be honest, I'm surprised you haven't shown up before now. I had a call from a Detective Ziebold in Hopeful the other day, and he told me that she—" he pointed to me, "—can require a lot of time."

I huffed, "If you call helping him solve cases a time-waster."

"Let me be clear. He didn't say you wasted his time. In fact, he was quite complimentary. Now, what's going on?"

"Have you had a chance to review the surveillance DVDs?"

He nodded. "That's why we brought in James McGregor. He left that night, and he came back in pretty sad shape. We figure he may have been drinking heavily out of remorse from killing his step-mother."

"Or, having been kind of an idiot, he went somewhere to drown his sorrows, and she was killed while he was gone. Did you notice the dark SUV that drove slowly around the house?" I crossed my legs.

"It didn't stop."

"It didn't stop within the camera's reach. It may have parked out of view."

"Maybe it was someone old who has trouble seeing in the dark. We don't have the manpower to chase everything that seems odd."

Patty smirked. "You don't need to waste your resources; we already know who was in the car. It was Katie Glass."

"And how would you know that?"

"Matilda told us."

He wrote in his book and then looked up. "That doesn't necessarily mean it was Katie's car. It could have been someone else's."

I leaned forward. "Katie admitted it. She told us she drove by that night to apologize for doubting who Patrick was. She also said when she didn't see Helen's light on, she didn't stop."

"If she didn't stop, she couldn't have killed Helen."

"Unless she's lying. Her theater is in dire need of a cash infusion, and she thought Helen had changed her will and left a legacy for her to manage." I examined my nails.

He made another note. "What else?"

Patty sat straighter. "Matilda. There's something funny going on with the household accounts. My husband asked her about it, and she said Helen asked her to donate food to a foster care facility. We called all the ones we could find, and none of them accept food donations."

He scribbled on his pad.

Patty cleared her throat. "That one's a bit touchy. We'd like to keep Matilda on, if she's not a murderer, and if you question her, she's going to know we suspect her."

He groaned. "Then how would you like me to proceed?"

"Just be gentle about it." She bit her lip.

I stood. "Thanks for your time, Lieutenant."

"That's it? No other suspects?"

"Not right now." Patty rose, shook his hand, and we strolled from the station. "I wish we could bring James out with us."

I slid into the car. "We've done what we can. It's in the police's hands now."

* * *

Patrick and the girls reclined on the chaise lounges, and a half-empty pitcher of pink lemonade sat on the table next to an insulated bucket of ice. I headed straight for it, filled two glasses with ice, and poured. I handed one to Patty. "Salud."

She sipped. "Ooh. Nice and tart with just a hint of sugar."

"How did it go?" Patrick shaded his eyes as he looked up.

"Fine." Patty motioned for him to move his legs, and she sat at the end of the chaise.

I dragged over a chair. "At least we've given them other suspects to chew on."

Matilda walked through the kitchen door. "Will James be joining us for dinner?"

Patty's gaze went to Patrick. He shook his head. "I don't think we should plan on it."

"Very well. It should be ready in about thirty minutes. Would you like it out here? Or in the dining room."

"Let's have it out here. That way, we can swim afterward."

Matilda left, and Patty and I stood. Patty said, "We'll change and come back down in a few minutes."

We trotted up the stairs, and I held my hand out to stop Patty before she turned into her room. "Do you think it's safe to eat dinner?"

"Not funny." She shut the door.

CHAPTER 21

Patrick

We called early the next morning to catch the kids at home. Patty leaned against me, pulled up the covers, and pressed speaker. Her mother answered, and the kids tripped over each other to tell us what was going on. Her mother laughed, "Whoa. One at a time."

Shawn said, "Mr. Jenson took us to another baseball game last night. They had hot dogs for a dime. He said I'd have a tummy ache if I had more than three."

"That was probably good advice," I said.

There was a scuffle, and our youngest said, "When are you coming home, Mommy? We miss you."

"I miss you too, sweetheart. Mommy and Daddy will be home just as soon as we can."

"But when?"

Her mother said, "Don't you like being with Grandma and Grandpa?"

He sniffled. "I want you to tuck me in and read me bedtime stories. You do it better."

"I'll call you tonight and read you a story."

He wailed, and loud footsteps became softer. Jane said, "He's run up to his room. I should go after him. Love you."

Tears ran down Patty's face. "Love you too."

I said, "Bye, boys. Be good for your Grandma. I'll talk to you soon." I pulled Patty closer. "It's okay, we'll be home soon, and they'll forget all about this."

"I need to get back there. Maybe if we can get the detective to say you're no longer a suspect, we can leave." She wiped her face with the back of her hand. "I can't leave you here by yourself."

I rubbed her arm. "I don't want to leave while James is in jail."

"We'll give it another few days and then we'll need to have a serious discussion. I feel like I've abandoned my family."

I kissed the top of her head. "You shower first. I'll text Rob and thank him for taking them out."

I picked up my phone and texted Rob: "Thanks for taking the kids to the ball games."

"No problem. Fun."

Louisa tapped on the door, opened it, and set the coffee down on the dresser. "Might get some rain today."

"Hope it's not like the gully-washer we had when I first arrived."

She laughed. "Early summer in Phoenix. Got to expect it. Would you like anything else?"

I shook my head, and she turned to leave. "Louisa, how did you like working for Helen?"

"Fine. She was a lovely lady. And, nice to Phillipe and me."

"I'm glad. It's important to like where you work."

She hesitated by the door. "Matilda might have felt differently."

"How so?" I mixed cream into my cup.

"I shouldn't say."

My eyebrow arched, and the shower stopped.

Her eyes darted to the bathroom door. "They fought, sometimes. About money. It had gotten worse lately."

She hurried out the bedroom door just as Patty came from the bathroom. "Oh, good. Coffee."

"Not just coffee. Java with a side of gossip."

* * *

Jenny, Cindy, and Merry sat at the dining room table. Cindy was reaching for a bagel when we walked through the door. "Scrambled eggs with chorizo this morning."

I stuck my head into the kitchen. "Two more, please, Matilda."

I poured two coffees, handed Patty one, and sat. "Rob's been great with the kids. I'll have to do something nice for him when we get back."

"I talked to him this morning. He's having as much fun as the kids are." Merry spread orange marmalade on her toast.

Matilda set down two platters on the table, eggs glistening. "I need to take some time off this afternoon."

"That's fine." I scooped eggs on my plate. "You've been working hard with all of us here. I hope you have something fun planned."

"Uh." Matilda backed up.

My eyes met hers. "I'm sorry. I shouldn't have asked. None of my business. In fact, we can fend for ourselves this evening."

"That's n-n-nice of you." She stuttered.

Patty rose. "Are you okay, Matilda?"

"No." Matilda sank onto the chair next to the sideboard. "The police want to see me. I can't imagine why. I told them everything I knew the last time."

Merry said, "I'm sure they're just extra thorough. Do you have an attorney?"

"Why would I need a lawyer? I haven't done anything wrong." Matilda put her hand to her heart.

"Never a bad idea," I said.

She paled. "My nephew is an attorney. I'll call him." She stood and strode into the kitchen, pulling her phone from her apron.

CHAPTER 22

Merry

After my second conference call, I decided it was time for a break. Rising from the chair, I put my arms over my head and bent to get a stretch in my lower back. I had been doing too much sitting. I opened the door, padded across the living room, and into the kitchen in search of coffee. Matilda sat on one of the stools, seeming to stare into space. I approached her. "Matilda? Are you okay?"

She jumped. "Merry, I didn't hear you come in."

"Are you okay?" I repeated.

She shook her head. "I've never been involved with the police before."

"Did you call your nephew?"

"He's going to meet me there at two. He said not to say anything if I get there before him." She looked up at me. "Nice people don't have this happen to them."

I poured coffee into a mug and then sat on the other stool. "Care to talk about it?"

Her eyes darted, and she stood. "I probably should get going. I don't want to be late."

* * *

"How did the trade show go? I saw you had some good pictures online. I didn't even know there was such a thing as a plumbing convention."

Rob said, "It was a nice boost for the local economy. Ann from the Pickled Herring said they know how to hoist a few. And, Ed said the sales receipts at the café were up twenty percent."

"That's great news. Before I forget, Patty and Patrick are thankful for all you've done for the boys."

"You can tell the kids are overwhelming her mom and dad a bit. They're not used to caring for three kids twenty-four-seven with that much energy. It's been fun for me. You never know what's going to come out of their mouths."

I put Rob on speaker and slid off my sandals. "Do tell."

"We went to the zoo, and a sloth was hanging from one of the branches."

"And?"

"Their youngest said, 'That can't be a sloth.' And, I said, 'Why not?' His answer was, 'Cindy calls me a sloth all the time. But he's ugly, and I'm cute.'"

I chuckled. "At least he has a good sense of self."

"The oldest has a good arm. He had a little league game the other day, and his team won."

"Sounds like you're getting along well." I changed into shorts.

"I'm not going to lie. Most nights, I've gotten home, and I'm whipped. They keep you running." He paused. "Have...have you thought any more about the possibility of us having children?"

I paused in the middle of wiping mascara from my eyes. My crow's feet were getting more pronounced. And, that line in my forehead was stark. Had it been there yesterday?

"Are you still there?"

"How important is it for you to have your own child?" I held my breath, waiting for his reply.

"Not as important as having you and Jenny in my life. I've thought long and hard about this. I'd love to have children, but not at the expense of our relationship."

I exhaled. "I love you, Rob."

"I love you too. We'll talk more about it when you get home. Do you have any idea when that might be?"

"Let me bring you up to speed on what's happened here." I did.

"So, Katie's a suspect because she needs the money for the theater, Matilda, because money's gone missing, and James is a little too fond of the high-life?"

"I'm not sure that's fair about James. He seems nice enough, but you're right, he's been quite clear Helen was his ticket to financial prosperity."

"Did the police let Matilda go?"

"Not sure. We had dinner out tonight, so I guess if she doesn't show up tomorrow, we can assume she's still with the police."

Rob yawned. "It's late, and I told the kids I'd pick them up early tomorrow to take them for pancakes."

"I love you, Rob Jenson."

"And, I you." He hung up.

Did I want more kids? What would Jenny think? Was I even capable of having them now? I groaned. It was too much to think about for one evening. I strolled out the door and down to the pool. The volleyball net was up, and James was in the middle of spiking the ball on Patrick. My mouth opened.

Patty grabbed my hand. "You're catching flies."

I sat next to her. "When did he get out?"

"He came home after you went to call Rob. His lawyer had to surrender his passport, but the judge decided he was a low-risk runner."

There was a bucket of beer in ice on the table, I fished out a bottle and held it up. "Want one?"

"Why not?"

I handed it to her and twisted the cap off mine. A cheer went up as Cindy got one past James. "Looks like a competition."

"None of them like to lose."

I sipped the beer. "What would you think of me having another child?"

"Why would you?" She turned toward me, and her eyes widened. "You're serious."

"I am. Rob wants to have a child of his own. I can't figure out if it's the right thing to do. Jenny will be going away to school; Drew is out of my life, even though his mess continues. And I'm old."

She laughed. "You're not old. We're the same age, and I'm certainly not old."

"I'm going to be forty this year. If I have a child, I'll be in my late fifties by the time he or she turns eighteen. Is that fair?"

"You'll be ancient." She clicked her bottle to mine. "You have to decide what's best for you and Rob. We had an eight-year gap between Cindy and Shawn, and I had accepted the fact she would probably be an only child. But look what happened, we ended up with four. And, I wouldn't give up one nanosecond with any one of them."

Jenny's blond ponytail bobbed as she dove for the ball. I leaned forward. "When Drew and I married, I wanted three or four kids. We had Jenny, and I was so happy. And then, life intervened. I love Jenny, and we've been a two-person team against the world."

"You've already opened your circle to include Rob. Maybe there's enough room for one more."

I laid my head back and stared at the stars. "Maybe. It seems kind of silly to worry about it till the annulment comes through."

✳ ✳ ✳

No coffee was magically delivered to the room. I focused, pouring all my energy into willing it to appear. *Drat.* I sighed and pushed myself from the bed. I guess Louisa wasn't here. After showering, I moseyed down the stairs.

Patty and James bent over the coffee machine. She said, "I think it's this button here."

"No. See, you have to put the water in here and then push that button."

Patty pushed her hair back from her face. "This shouldn't be so complicated."

"I come bearing gifts." Patrick pushed open the kitchen door and held up a large box of coffee with a spout.

"Thank goodness." I sank onto a kitchen stool.

"And, donuts." He put the box on the island.

"Coffee first." James filled four mugs.

"Salvation." I smelled and then drank. "This is silly. We're four adults who don't have help at home. How can this be so hard?"

Patrick said, "Not hard at all—just required a trip and a credit card."

"What are we going to do when we get home? We've been so spoiled here." Patty sat next to me.

Louisa strolled in the kitchen door. She jumped when she saw us. "Where's Matilda?"

"Not sure," Patrick said.

She eyed the container on the counter. "Are we out of coffee?"

James sighed, "We couldn't figure out the machine."

"Didn't Matilda tell you I'd be late this morning?" Louisa shifted from foot to foot.

"It must have slipped her mind." Patrick pushed his mug away. "No problem. Can you show us how to work it?"

Louisa bustled to the machine and gave us a tutorial. When she finished, there was an awkward pause. "Do you know what time Matilda will be in?"

Patrick shook his head.

"Okay. Well, I better get on with the rooms." She edged out the door.

"That was awkward." Patty topped off her mug.

Jenny and Cindy ran in. "What's for breakfast?" Cindy asked.

"Ooh. Donuts." Jenny opened the box, then paused. "Where's Matilda?"

* * *

Everybody went their own way after breakfast. I claimed the office and was quickly ensconced, making calls. Around eleven, the house phone rang. I let it ring a few times, hoping someone else would answer; no such luck. I picked it up. "Hello?"

"Hi Merry, it's Matilda. They let me go late yesterday, and I was too exhausted to come in this morning. Is Patrick there?"

"Let me find him."

I walked to the library and opened the door. James looked up. I asked, "You don't know where Patrick is, do you?"

He shook his head, so I shut the door, pulled out my phone, and texted Patrick.

"Hey, Merry? I picked it up. You can hang up now."

I walked back to the office, hung up the phone, and got back to work.

* * *

Two hours later, my stomach grumbled. I closed my laptop, walked to the kitchen, and opened the door. Patty was cooking shrimp in a frying pan and had salad fixings spread on the table.

I said, "I'm glad someone felt industrious."

"Patrick ran out for the salad stuff; I just put it in bowls." She held up the pan. "I found these in the freezer and thought it would be good to add protein."

"Works for me. Where are we eating?"

"By the pool. I put the misters on. Can you grab the dressing and iced tea from the fridge and put it on the island? I figured it would be easier if everyone filled their plates here."

"I'll let James know. Where is everybody?"

She shrugged. "Just text them."

I sent a group note, walked back to the library, and opened the door. James jumped.

"Sorry, didn't mean to startle you, I texted everyone else but didn't have your number. Lunch is ready."

He put papers in a folder and shoved them under his laptop. "I'm starved."

I waited.

He rose and extended his hand. "After you. Did you find Patrick this morning?"

"I did."

We walked into the kitchen where Patrick was piling shrimp on top of his salad.

"What did Matilda want?" I asked.

"She wanted to know if she should cook dinner this evening."

"What did you tell her?"

He hesitated. "I told her to come back tomorrow."

My eyebrow lifted. "You're keeping her on?"

"At least till we know what happened. Plus, you saw how helpless we are in the morning."

"Tough choice. Lap of luxury versus being killed in our sleep." Patty shoved the door open with her hip and glanced toward the girls sitting outside. "Mums the word."

*　*　*

I dozed on and off. I kept thinking about Rob and the impact of having another child would make on my life. He was a good man and would be such a good father. Would it be fair to deny him the opportunity? *Although, if kids were that important to him, shouldn't he have had them earlier?* I turned over and pounded my pillow. Not that I would have wanted him to find someone else. I turned over again. Pink glowed around the plantation shutters. It would be dawn soon, I groaned. *I might as well get up.*

I threw on shorts and a t-shirt and wandered downstairs. No light shone under the kitchen door. *That's strange, shouldn't Matilda be here?* I pushed it open and switched on the light. Matilda had been sitting on a stool in the corner and put a hand up to shield her eyes.

I jumped. "I didn't realize anyone was here." I walked closer to her. Are you all right? Why are you sitting in the dark?"

She was pale, her hair was disheveled, and she was rubbing her hands up and down on her pants. "I don't know what to do. I need this job."

I retrieved a glass, filled it with water, and set it down in front of her. "What happened?"

She gulped the water. "Thanks."

"Maybe you better tell me what's going on." I pulled another stool over and sat.

"I can't. I'll lose my job." She shuddered. "I guess it doesn't matter now; they're just going to find out from the police anyway. My nephew made me tell them."

I tilted my head and waited.

"The last two years have been difficult. My mother has early-stage Alzheimer's, and about three months ago, it became too hard to care for her, especially since I had to work." Tears ran down her face. "I decided she'd have to leave home. It was the most difficult decision I've ever made. My sisters were no help. They left everything to me."

I stood, retrieved the tissue box from over the sink, and handed it to her.

"Thanks. She's still with it most of the time, so she knew what I was doing. The looks she gave me. The arguments." Matilda shook her head. "She didn't have any money, so she was eligible for Medicaid. But they only pay if she goes into a nursing home. I just couldn't do that to her. Not yet. Within the next year or so, her disease will progress to the point where I'll have to, but for now, I chose a nice assisted living facility. It's cheerful and sunny.

"They have musical programs and other brain-stimulating activities." She stood and poured more water, staring out onto the grounds. "It's expensive. I had savings, so I've been using that. It wasn't going to be enough. Helen had so much, and my mother so little."

She turned and gasped, "I'm not proud of it, but I started taking money from the household accounts. Helen didn't even notice. Until about a month ago. Her accountant did an audit and asked if she knew how much she was spending on food. She was shocked, and of course, she came to me.

"I explained what happened. We argued. Helen told me she needed to think about what to do, but to be frank, it became uncomfortable working here. I thought I would lose my job. But the worst case was that she'd turn me in to the police. Then she was killed."

She wiped her eyes. "That's what I told the police. And, now I'm going to have to tell the Twilligers. I'm so ashamed, and I need this job. I lied to them. I told them I was giving food to a foster care agency. What are they going to think of me?"

I touched her arm. "Matilda, if you don't mind me asking, how much did Helen leave you in her will?"

She blew her nose. "Seventy-five thousand. It should be enough." Her eyes wandered. "What should I do?"

"First things first. What were you planning on for breakfast?"

"Cinnamon rolls." Her eyes lifted to the clock. "Need to get going."

"Why don't I get started, and you take a few minutes to freshen up?"

She handed me a recipe card. "I'll be right back."

CHAPTER 23

Patrick

Louisa tapped on the door, opened it, and placed a tray on the dresser. "Good morning," she said as she eased back out the door.

I rose, walked to the pot, and poured two mugs. "It's good to have things back to normal."

"More cream, please," Patty said. "How can you say normal? The only thing that would make this complete is if Katie lived here. That way, we'd have all three suspects living under our roof."

"Four." I handed her a mug.

She kissed my shoulder as I settled back in bed. "Three. I know you didn't do it."

We sat there for a few minutes in silence. "I'm going to have to talk to her."

"Katie?"

"Matilda. She lied to us. I can't let this go without further conversation." I blew on the mug. "Should James be there?"

"Up to him."

"We're going to have to go back home soon, and I don't know how I feel about Matilda having free reign of the house while we're gone."

"Plus, do you need a full-time cook if we're not here?" Patty stood and opened the blinds.

"Maybe I could rent the place."

"You want to be an absentee landlord? Look, Helen left a trust to pay for the running of the household, you just inherited a million dollars, and this place takes a lot of upkeep. Let's not jump into things; you have plenty of time to make decisions."

I pulled her onto my lap. "I'm so glad I married you."

"But you're right, you need to have a conversation with Matilda." Her finger bopped my nose.

"I will," I groaned.

We dressed and made our way downstairs. The scent of cinnamon permeated the house. I took Patty's hand. "Something smells good."

Cindy and Jenny were already in the dining room, drinking orange juice. Cindy said, "Miss Matilda and Mrs. March are making cinnamon rolls, they said they'd be ready in twenty."

"Why is Merry helping Matilda?" Patty picked up the pitcher and poured us juice.

"Maybe she missed baking." Jenny shrugged.

Merry pushed open the kitchen door. "Oh good, you're up. Do you have a minute?" She pointed toward the living room. Patty and I followed her. "Let's get James too. He's in the library. On second thought, let's join him there."

I rapped on the library door and opened it. "Mind if we join you?"

James extended his hand. "Please do."

We filed in and sat.

"I had a long conversation with Matilda." Merry filled us in.

I leaned back in the chair and whistled. "So, she took the money to pay for her mother's care?"

"That's right." Merry rubbed the back of her neck.

"How do we know it's true? The first story wasn't. She had us calling all over Phoenix." Patty grumbled.

"She gave me the name of the facility, called them, and gave them permission to talk to me. I did. Her mother's been there for three months. It checked out, and I'm sure the police will check too."

"What a position to be in. I feel bad for her, having to make those kinds of choices," I said.

"I just wished she had told us the truth the first time around." Patty sat on the sofa.

"Matilda's always been nice to me. Seems kind of harsh she's in this bind because she was trying to do the right thing for her mother," James said.

"You think it's okay she stole from Helen?" I turned toward him.

"She was in a bind. We have plenty of money. I think you should just chill."

I frowned. "Helen trusted her, and Matilda stole from her."

"She knew about it for a month and didn't fire her. If Helen was okay with it, why aren't we?"

Patty interjected, "They argued about it, so I'm not sure Helen was 'okay.' And, if Matilda did it once, she could do it again."

"Unless you put safeguards in place." James deposited his computer in a carrying case.

I rubbed my chin. "That's an idea. I could give her a debit card to use from a separate account that gets replenished monthly. If she needed more than that, she'd have to let me know what it was for." I paused. "Of course, it still seems silly to pay for a chef when we're not here a lot."

"I've meant to talk to you about that. Do you think my kids and I could use it a few times a year when you and Patty aren't here?" James stood.

I laughed. "Of course. Now that you mention it, it might be a good idea to have all of us here together once a year."

"That would be nice," Patty said.

"Between our families, any friends you let stay, and if you let Katie continue to use it for fundraisers, we may be able to keep Matilda busy." James opened the door.

"Thanks for the suggestions. I need to talk to Matilda today, so I'll think about it. You don't want to join me, do you?"

"To dress down Matilda? Nope. Not my house." He smiled and clapped me on the back. "C'mon, people. There's sugar with my name on it."

* * *

At breakfast, Matilda skittered in and out of the kitchen, hardly saying a word and jumping at the slightest sound. Afterward, I met with her in the kitchen. We agreed her employment would continue for the time being, and that, before I left, I would take her credit card and issue a debit card.

Her face regained some color, and she pulled iced tea from the fridge. "Would you like some? It's blackberry."

I nodded.

"What about the police?"

"I'll tell them we've decided not to press charges. I know your nephew told you they might decide to proceed anyway, but hopefully, they'll listen to us."

She grinned from ear to ear as she handed me the tea. "I can't tell you how much I appreciate this. Not everyone would be as nice."

I took the glass from her and meandered into the living room, where Patty was reading a book.

She moved her feet from the couch. "How did it go?"

"She was glad we're not firing her, and that I'm going to tell the police we're not pressing charges."

"I hope it was the right thing to do."

"Time will tell. Where are the girls?"

"Helping Phillipe gather limes from the trees. They wanted fresh limeade."

"That sounds good. I think I'll help." I followed the laughter coming from behind the house and to the left. Phillipe balanced on a rickety old ladder whose wood was bleached almost white from the sun. He was tossing limes to the girls, who were catching them and depositing them in a burlap sack.

Cindy waved. "Help us, Dad."

Phillipe tossed one to me. I caught it and said to Cindy, "Go long."

She ran a route. I threw it, and she nabbed it without difficulty.

"One more." I motioned to Phillipe, and he laughed and under-armed me another. I gestured to the other side.

Cindy took off and had to dive for it by an oleander. One of the branches broke. She held up the lime, celebrating. "Didn't even hit the ground."

I rushed toward her. "Are you okay? I didn't mean to throw it that far."

She glanced at her arm. "It's just a scratch."

"You should probably wash it, just in case."

"Cindy, I think we have enough. Thanks, Mr. Phillipe!" Jenny walked into the house.

Cindy followed her, and I brought up the rear. Jenny handed Matilda the limes and said, "I'll help."

They started juicing the limes, and I went to find Cindy. She was washing her scratch in the half bath.

"Can you get it?"

"I'm not a kid, Dad."

"It looks a little red."

"It's fine."

"Do you want a bandage?"

She huffed and stalked into the kitchen.

Patty looked up as Cindy passed. "What's that all about?"

I sat next to her on the sofa. "Our little girl is growing up."

"We've decided not to press charges." I sat, once again, in a hard wooden chair at the Police Station.

Detective Schwartz leaned back, and his fingers moved into a steeple position. "I'm not sure that's wise. You do know she's under suspicion in Mrs. McGregor's murder?"

"I'm aware of that."

"She must be a heck of a cook."

I nodded. "One other thing."

His eyebrow rose.

"We have three young boys at home, and I think my wife's parents are getting a bit stressed caring for them. My boss is also asking when I'll be coming home. I sell cars for a living and work on commission. You told me not to leave town. With all of these other suspects, would it be possible for me to leave?"

He shook his head. "I would think you'd want to know who killed your mother."

"You could call me to let me know when you've found the guilty party."

"I'm not releasing you yet."

"Did you talk to Katie Glass? She was in the vicinity of the house the night of the murder."

"This is an open investigation. I can't comment on it."

"I'm not a reporter. I'm the victim's son. We've been cooperating and bringing you information. I think you could share a little."

He sighed. "It was her car. She admitted it. But she said she didn't stop. She stuck to her story that when she didn't see Helen's light, she drove on. Thanks for coming in, Mr. Twilliger. I'll let you know when you can leave town." He stood. "And, let me know if you change your mind about pressing charges."

I left the station and called Patty from the car. "No luck on leaving. I'm stuck here."

Patty groaned. "When will you be home?"

"I'm about five minutes out. Do you need me to stop for anything?"

"Nope. See you in a few."

"Don't speak" by No Doubt came on the radio, and I cranked the volume. I wish I knew what all the people involved in this mess had really done. It would be nice to know who was telling the truth. I pulled into the drive. I needed to think about returning the rental too. Charges were starting to add up.

As I walked into the house, Patty held paint swatches against the wall, her head tilted. I came up from behind and kissed her neck. "What are you doing?"

"Thinking about repainting this room. I thought a lighter color might brighten it up."

"I thought you liked it."

Her head tilted the other way as she held up another color. "I do. But since it's our house, I might as well make improvements."

I groaned. "Where are the girls?"

She pointed toward the pool. The volleyball net was up, and Cindy was mid-spike. Patty walked closer to the window. "What's wrong with her arm?"

We moved toward the pool in unison.

I opened the door. "Cindy, what's on your arm?"

She twisted to examine it. Angry red blisters ran in a line across her upper arm. "Doesn't hurt much."

Patty gestured. "Come here."

She paddled to the side of the pool and extended her arm. "See? It's not too bad."

"That's where you got scratched. It shouldn't blister like that. Maybe it's infected. Get out, I'm going to take you to the doctor."

Cindy groaned. "We're in the middle of a game. Do we have to?"

"Yes."

She clambered out. "Back soon."

"Want me to come?" Jenny asked.

"I'll be fine." Cindy dried herself off, wrapped the towel around her suit, and ran up the stairs.

Jenny plopped onto a chaise and raised the umbrella, and I pulled out my keys. "I can take her."

Patty shook her head. "I'll go."

* * *

Two hours later, the garage door opened, and Patty and Cindy walked into the living room. I stood. "What happened?"

"She's fine. They gave us salve. It wasn't an infection; it's a reaction to the oleander. They're poisonous, so we'll be staying away from them. When the boys come, we'll need to declare that area off-limits."

I hugged Cindy, being careful to avoid the blisters. "I'm sorry about that throw."

"Have Miss Matilda make me a chocolate shake and grilled cheese for lunch, and we're good."

"Done." I headed toward the kitchen.

Matilda was rolling pie dough. She looked up when I walked through the door.

"The girls would like chocolate shakes and grilled cheese sandwiches for lunch."

"No problem. Tell them I'll work on that as soon as I get this dough finished and resting in the fridge."

"One more thing."

She laid a stencil on the top crust and used a sharp knife to cut the outline.

"I spoke with the police this morning. I told them we had decided not to press charges on the theft."

Her eyes teared as she continued cutting the pattern. "Thank you, sir. I can't tell you how much that means to me."

"Just remember what we talked about."

She wiped her eye with the back of her hand. "I won't forget."

I went back to the living room, where Patty was leafing through a pattern book on the sofa. I sat next to her. "What's this?"

"If we're going to go to all the trouble of painting, we should think about reupholstering these sofas. And, maybe that chair over there. What do you think of this pattern to punch things up?"

I rubbed the back of my neck.

CHAPTER 24

Merry

The next day, Patty and I decided to go out to lunch to a fifties-themed diner with an abundance of stainless steel, white counters, and red faux leather booths. The hostess sat us, and Patty groaned. "I can't believe how slow the police are. This is a big town; I'm starting to wonder if smaller towns are better."

I lifted my lemonade. "You know that small towns are."

"But don't these people have more resources?"

"They also have more crimes. I read in the paper Fentanyl deaths are exploding here. That means the coroners are also backed up. At least we found out how she died."

"I guess. It's frustrating they still haven't pinned down the exact time." Patty frowned.

The waitress came to the table. "Are you ready to order?"

Patty pointed to the hot dog. "I'm in the mood for something plain. Would you please tell them to add sauerkraut and onions and maybe a jalapeno or two? And fries. I need fries."

"Plain?" I snorted.

She gave me a dirty look. "Just order."

"I'll have the house salad with shrimp. Dressing on the side, please."

The waitress walked away, still writing.

Patty put her napkin in her lap. "At least the décor is nice."

"I'm glad you suggested lunch." I played with the silverware and then looked up. "I'm sorry, but I can't stay much longer. Some clients like that personal touch, and we have the appreciation event coming up. Cheryl and the rest of the team are doing a great job, but I feel like I've abandoned them."

"You've worked at least part of every day."

"I know. But it's not the same. It'd be different if I could see an end in sight."

The waitress set a large platter down, which held Patty's fully dressed hot dog and what seemed like ten potatoes worth of fries. Then she put my salad in front of me.

Patty turned the fry part of her plate toward me. "Feel free."

"I feel guilty even talking to you about this. You need me."

"You're a great friend. I don't know many people who'd leave their lives and fly across the country to help." She sighed.

"I'm not leaving yet." I pulled a pad from my purse. There were three things listed: James's bar, papers, and Katie's friend. I pointed to the first. "We need to visit the bar James went to, second, when I was looking for Patrick the other day, James was cagey and stuck papers under his computer, and third, we need to find out who the guy was who came up to Katie during the reception after Helen's funeral. I think his name was Gerard."

"What papers, and why do we need to find Gerard?" Patty dunked a fry in catsup.

"I'm not sure what the papers are. The way James acted was suspicious. You know that look the kids give you when they've done something wrong, and they're hoping you don't find out?"

"My kids wrote the book on that."

"Something very fishy." I took another fry. "I was hoping this would be a low-cal lunch. It won't be if I keep eating these."

"And Katie's friend?"

"He knows something. I'm sure of it."

* * *

"Who would name a bar 'Seedy's?'" Patty pulled into the parking lot.

I pointed to the squat building with nary a window. "It kind of fits."

"You really want to go in?" She slid her purse strap across her chest. "I'm not leaving my purse hanging from the back of a chair in a place like this."

"Let's go." I pushed open the door to the bar and was assailed by stale cigarette smoke. The five occupants of the small bar turned toward us, all pale older men who gripped the drinks in front of them like they were afraid it might be their last. I nodded, trying to be friendly, but my shoes made small sucking sounds as I walked toward the bar. I couldn't help but grimace. *At least I wore sneakers.*

Patty climbed onto the stool next to me as the bartender strode toward us. He looked to be in his sixties with a wiry frame, two-day-old beard, and wispy comb-over. "What can I get you, ladies?"

Patty blurted, "Beer. In a bottle."

"Bud okay?"

She nodded.

"Make that two," I said.

He popped the tops, set them in front of us, and leaned against the back of the bar. "New to town?"

"Visiting." Patty took a swig.

His eyebrow rose. "Don't take this the wrong way, but you two don't look like you get out to bars much."

She straightened in her chair. "There's a bar in the town we live in that we go to all the time. 'The Pickled Herring.'"

"Sounds like a frou-frou place."

"It's not. It has the most wonderful mahogany bar with brass accents, a lovely mirror, and quaint wooden tables—"

He snorted. "Just as I thought. Now don't get me wrong, I'm appreciative of the business and all, but what are you really doing here?"

I put my hand on Patty's arm to stop her from answering. "We wanted to ask you a few questions."

"You lawyers?" He rubbed the bar in front of us with what could have been a white cloth in a different century.

Patty laughed. "I'm a decorator, and she owns an insurance shop in our small town."

"What kind of insurance? My pops was an insurance agent for a property and casualty company."

"I sell a broad range of products, including property and casualty." I smiled.

"Well, what do you know? My old man was a great guy, and everyone in town admired him." He extended his hand, "Bud Seely."

I shook it. "Glad to meet you, Bud."

"What do you need to know? I'm always willing to help an insurance agent."

"Someone said they had been here the other week. That person looked like they got pretty drunk."

"I don't overserve." He tossed the cloth behind him. "Most of my clientele have a few before they get here."

Patty put her thumb on her phone to unlock it and scrolled to a picture she had taken of James, Patrick, and Cindy and handed it to him. "The guy on the left, James."

"Yeah. I remember him. He's the guy the police were asking about."

"What did they want to know?" She took her phone back and put it in her purse.

"If he was here, that kind of thing."

"What did you tell them?" I sipped my beer.

"He got here around eleven. I remember because he was better dressed than the people who normally come here and because the game had just finished. Jack—" he pointed to a portly man by himself in a corner, "had lost a bundle—you said his name was James?"

I nodded.

"He seemed like an okay guy, talking baseball and all, but after a few beers, he started spouting off about the big plans he had for his life. He was going to own thoroughbreds and win the Kentucky Derby.

"I asked him how he was going to accomplish that. He got cagey. Said he wouldn't be surprised if he came into money in the not so distant future. Then Bob, over there, challenged him. He said if James was going to be so flush, wouldn't he want to buy them all a drink in advance of his good fortune. James laughed and bought shots for everyone."

Patty's face paled. "He said he was going to come into money?"

"He did. The lads talked him into one last round, and he obliged. I took his keys and poured him into a cab when the bar closed at two."

"How did he get his car back?" I drank the dregs of my beer.

"Came back the next day for his keys with some guy in a minivan. Want another?" He pointed at the bottle. "On the house."

I shook my head. "Thanks, but we need to be getting back."

Patty stood, and we squished our way out the door. She turned to me. "I'm glad I brought the rental instead of Helen's car. We're going to have to use a firehose on the bottoms of our shoes."

Patrick was pacing in the hall when we returned. "What took you so long? I was starting to get worried." His nose wrinkled. "You smell like you live in a brewery."

"You're lucky we left our sneakers outside." Patty stretched to kiss him on the cheek. "Shower first. Where are the girls and James?"

"Girls are watching a movie in the theater room, and James is in the library."

"Tell James we need to talk to him once we've showered." Patty grabbed two trash bags from the kitchen and handed one to me. "Put your clothes in this. We'll leave them in the laundry tonight."

I walked into my room, stripped, and jumped into the shower. The stench from the bar was soon replaced by the light floral scent of the shampoo and body wash. I sighed. *Need to figure out how to get these toiletries at home.* A quick scrub with almond oil soap and I was done. I put on clean shorts and a shirt, and almost ran into Patty when I opened the door to the hallway. Neither of us had taken the time to dry our hair. She took my garbage bag and said, "I'll dump this with mine."

I sat across from Patrick, and James stood by the fireplace, looking as if he was poised to make a quick exit. He asked, "What's this about?"

Patty walked back into the room and sank onto the sofa next to Patrick. "Merry and I visited Seedy's tonight."

"Doesn't seem like your kind of place," he laughed.

She shuddered. "It isn't. But, we wanted to find out more about what happened the night that Helen died."

He walked to the mini-fridge and pulled out a beer. "I think I'm going to need one of these. Anyone else?"

Patrick nodded. James gave him one and said, "What did you hear?"

I sat back on the sofa and crossed my arms. "That you were spouting off, telling everyone how much money you were going to inherit in the not-too-distant future. And, why would you say that if you hadn't already killed Helen, or meant to kill her when you came back to the house?"

"You told them you were going to inherit? Did you kill her? Patrick's face reddened.

"Whoa, whoa, whoa!" James retreated, hands up. "I didn't kill her. It was stupid of me to open my mouth, I'm not going to deny that, but I just meant she was old and couldn't last forever."

"First, you tell us you didn't leave the house. Then you say you just went for a beer. And, now we find out you got trashed and were bragging about an inheritance. No wonder the police arrested you. I'm not sure I want you in this house anymore." Patrick's teeth clenched.

Cindy and Jenny, mouths open, tried to ease back through the kitchen door.

I jumped up. "Movie over already? Why don't you go upstairs, and we'll be there soon to say goodnight."

They raced across the room and up the stairs. Patty sighed. "That wasn't good."

James plunked down on a chair and ran his fingers through his hair. "I didn't do it. No matter what you think of me, I didn't. If you want me to leave, I'll go."

"I just want you to stop lying." Patrick sat on the sofa. "I want us to be like true brothers. And I want to be able to trust you."

"You can trust me. I've been telling the truth about important things."

Patty rolled her eyes.

"I went out that night, okay? You already know that. And, you know I could hardly stand up when I got back. You saw the video. I couldn't have killed Helen. I'm surprised she didn't wake up when I got back because I knocked that over," He pointed to a table by the vestibule near the garage.

* * *

Patty sat on the window seat, and I eased onto the end of Jenny's bed. Cindy said, "What's going on. Did Uncle James kill his step-mother?"

"I don't think so. I hope not," Patty said.

"He seems so nice." Cindy shivered.

"He is. That's why it's so hard to believe."

"Is he moving out?"

"Just to be on the safe side. He's going to stay at the hotel your father was in when he got here. Your dad asked your uncle for his key back."

Cindy turned on her side, away from Patty.

"Sometimes, we have to make tough decisions. This is one of those times." Patty rubbed her back in small slow circles.

"We don't want you alone with him until this is resolved." I stood.

Patty and I walked out the door. As I shut it, Cindy asked Jenny, "You don't think he did it do you? Who could kill their step-mother?"

I missed Jenny's reply. Patty and I stopped at my room, and I yawned. "It's been quite a day. Tomorrow will be busy too."

"Tomorrow?"

"We're going to find Gerard." I yawned again.

"I'll let you get to bed."

I shut my door and turned the lock.

Patty pushed the door open with her foot. "I bring coffee."

I sat behind Helen's desk. "Good, you're up. I had an early morning call and then hit the internet."

Patty poured coffee into my mug and sat the insulated carafe down on the desk. "Internet?"

"Finding Gerard. I looked at the theater site, and they had a 'Thanking Donors' page. There's a Gerard Wellbrook listed, plus he's on their Board. His picture is tiny, but I think it's him." I turned the iPad toward her. "What do you think?"

She picked it up and made the picture larger. That just made it blurrier. "Not the best photo. It could be him."

I took the computer back. "I searched his name, and there's a match on a guy who has a national chain of restaurants called "Grandma Mary's Comfort Food.""

"I went to one of those in Chicago. It was delicious."

"It's a public company—" I whistled "—that's doing very well. Maybe I should invest."

Patty tapped the table. "Let's stay on track. Is it him?"

I smiled and flipped the computer toward her.

"Much better picture. What's the plan?"

I held up my finger and dialed. "Hi, this is Meredith March. I was wondering if Mr. Wellbrook would have a few minutes today."

"He's got a very busy day. What is this in reference to?"

"My friend, Patty Twilliger and I met him at Helen McGregor's funeral, and we've been thinking about donating money to the Scottsdale Revival Theater—"

"I might be able to fit you in at two o'clock at the Grandma Mary's in Scottsdale."

"We'll see him then." I pressed end.

"We're going to donate money?" Patty's eyes widened.

"You know better than that."

"A little slow. Not much sleep last night."

CHAPTER 25

Merry

The girls wanted to read by the pool, and Patrick was going stir-crazy, so he decided to join our expedition to Grandma Mary's. The restaurant looked like it could seat a thousand people, and the entrance was through a huge green four-leaf clover. Patrick held the door for Patty and me, and I strode toward the host stand. "Meredith March and the Twilligers to see Gerard Wellbrook."

The man nodded and took us toward a circular table in the middle of the restaurant. The furniture was dominated by rustic wood, and on the far wall, there was a painting of a brown, craggy-topped mountain surrounded by emerald green grass. I walked toward it. "This is pretty."

Gerard walked through the automatic doors to my right as pots clanged behind him. "It's Mount Nephin. My grandmother was from County Cork." He extended his hand. "Gerard Wellbrook. I'm sorry we didn't meet the other week."

Patrick and Patty introduced themselves. Gerard held Patrick's hand a beat too long. "You look so like your father. But those blue eyes are your mother's. Katie told me you were Helen's son."

Patrick nodded. "Unfortunately, I only knew her for a few days, but she seemed like a very nice person."

"She was, and she is missed." He gestured toward the round table. "Shall we sit? Would you like something to drink?"

Patrick said, "Black and Tan."

"A man after my own heart." Gerard nodded at the waitress. "Two."

"I'll have an iced tea." Patty and I said in unison.

The waitress left, and another delivered Irish soda bread on a large plate. Gerard lifted the plate and said, "Ladies?"

I slid a piece of the soda bread off the plate, broke off a smaller chunk, and slathered it with butter. I popped it in my mouth. The first waitress returned with drinks and passed them around.

"Well, if you're going to—" Patty helped herself to the bread, and Patrick and Gerard followed suit.

"This is good. Nice and light, and I love the raisins," I said.

"Don't tell my mother, she'll disown me, but I think this may be better than hers." Patty spread butter on another piece.

"My grandmother's secret recipe." Gerard smiled. "I understand you're interested in donating to the Theater? Helen was such a great benefactor; it would be nice to see her legacy continued."

"Katie said Helen got involved in the theater about six years ago?" Patrick slid another slice of bread onto his plate.

Gerard tilted his head. "That sounds about right. I knew Helen and Frank for longer than that. We traveled in the same circles. For as big as it is, Phoenix is still a small town for people like us."

"People like you?"

"You know. People who invest in the arts." Gerard sipped his black and tan.

Patty asked, "Can you tell us more about what the theater will be using the money for?"

"Katie has a brochure that details—"

"We've seen that. But I find it's helpful to talk to someone in the know about what's really going on, and you seem to have your hand on the pulse of society here."

"I am pretty tied in." He leaned back in his chair, and a small smile played across his face.

"It was sad when Helen died. I got the impression Katie expected Helen's will to contain a bequest to the theater." Patty looked at him like Nancy Reagan used to look at Ronnie.

Gerard leaned toward her and lowered his voice. "I probably shouldn't say this, but Katie was stunned. She said Helen had told her repeatedly that she was going to leave a healthy sum to the theater, and Katie would have control over how the money would be spent. She thought she'd have clout. You know Katie grew up poor, right?"

Patty nodded.

"She thought she'd finally be one of us." He chuckled. "Katie's fun, but she doesn't realize you can't buy your way into the club; you have to be born to it. Otherwise, you're just a climber."

I bit my lip to control my temper and felt my face flush. Patrick's eyes grew large.

Patty laughed. "So true. One more thing. I guess you'll be able to tap quite a few donors to make up for the fact that Helen's legacy was a disappointment."

"Sadly, no. Many of us lost money when the bottom of the commercial market dropped out a decade or so ago. It was difficult. Katie's been doing great work fundraising and cultivating donors, but it won't be easy to replace Helen." He lifted his beer toward Patrick. "And that's where you come in. You can take Helen's place."

Patrick stood. "We'll have to think about it. Thanks for your candor and the information. I appreciate it."

Patty and I followed Patrick's lead, and Patty shook Gerard's hand. "It was good to get to know you better."

I gave a curt nod, and we left. The door shut behind me, I popped two antacids and turned to Patty. "How on earth could you be so calm?"

She shook her head. "Odious man, but he gave us good information. He confirmed that Katie thought the lock was in on the money, and that there doesn't seem to be anyone else who has the interest or the money to take Helen's place. The only thing that confuses me is why hadn't Helen changed her will?"

Patrick unlocked the car, and we climbed in. He pressed the starter. "That's true. The day after she met me, Helen said she was going to change her will, and she emailed her lawyer that night. Was she just stringing Katie along? Or did she think she had plenty of time to make the change?"

Patty rubbed his arm. "We'll probably never know."

* * *

When we got back to the house, I had a surprise waiting for me. Rob was sitting by the pool with the girls. I rushed into his arms. "What are you doing here?"

"I missed you. So I hopped a flight, and here I am." He kissed me.

"That's why you didn't answer my call."

"Didn't want to spoil the surprise." He hugged Patty and shook Patrick's hand. "Hope you don't mind me dropping in for a few days."

Patrick grinned. "No problem. You can have James's room."

"Where's James? Did the police take him into custody again?"

"I kicked him out. You've missed a few installments." Patrick eyed the girls. "Let's talk later."

I turned to Rob. "Up for a swim?"

"In this heat? Absolutely!"

"Where's your bag? I'll show you your room."

We walked up the stairs. He said, "Nice house. Could fit three of mine in here."

I laughed and opened the door to James's room. "This is it. Mine's down the other hall. It looks like Louisa's way ahead of us." Fresh flowers adorned the side table, and it looked like all of James's things had been put away.

Rob pulled me into his arms. "It's a shame we can't share the same room."

"Jenny's here."

He kissed me. "I know. Being here with you both is enough. I am feeling a bit guilty about Patty's parents. That's why I decided it'll only be a short stay."

"I'll meet you at the pool in fifteen." I gave him one last kiss. "So glad you're here."

I wandered down the hall to my room. I had missed Rob. Hugging him felt so good, so natural. I smiled as I changed into my bathing suit. Then, I paused as I strode past the mirror. I grabbed a pillow, stuffed it under my cover-up, and turned sideways. *Could I do this again? Morning sickness, bloating, nine months of not drinking.*

The door opened. "Mom, Matilda wants to know—what are you doing?"

The pillow slipped from under the cover-up and dropped to the floor. My face felt like it was on fire. "Nothing."

Her eyes traveled from the pillow to me and back to the pillow. "Are you pregnant?"

"No! Don't be silly." I put the pillow back on the bed.

"Then, what were you doing?" Her hand went to her hip.

"Sit down." I popped an antacid and sat on the bed.

She dropped down next to me. "You shouldn't be eating those all the time."

"I don't."

Jenny stared at me.

"Not all the time."

"What was with the pillow?"

I put my arm around her. "You know I'm waiting for the annulment to come through."

"So?"

"When it does, Rob and I will probably get married."

"I know that."

"What would you think if I had another child?" I tensed.

She stood. "Aren't you kind of old?"

"I'm not that old." I pulled on her hand, and she sat back down.

"I don't know how I'd feel. It'd be kind of neat to have a brother or sister. But on the other hand, I'll be away at school soon. Would I even know him or her? I'd be more of an aunt than a sister." She tucked her foot underneath her. "I'm not old enough to be an aunt. It's just weird. Would the baby get my room?"

I rubbed her back. "Your room will always be yours. Of course, who knows if we'll stay in that house?"

Jenny shuddered. "Too many changes. I have to think about this."

"It'll be okay. Nothing's going to happen overnight. I love you."

"I love you too, Mom." She hugged me. "Matilda wanted to know if we wanted dinner by the pool. Mrs. Twilliger said to ask you."

"Dinner by the pool sounds great."

✳ ✳ ✳

After dinner, the girls wanted to watch a movie we weren't interested in, so Patrick, Patty, Rob, and I retired to the living room. Patrick held up a bottle of Bailey's. "Anyone?"

There were nods all around, so he poured four glasses. Rob lifted his. "To finding out who killed Helen."

I curled up next to him on the sofa: Bay leaves, argan oil, and buttered rum. I had missed that smell. I moved even closer.

Patrick cleared his throat. "We could leave if you want the room to yourselves."

Rob laughed. "No need. We'll behave ourselves. "

"I'll be good." I backed away slightly.

"What's new with the case?" Rob asked.

Patty, Patrick, and I took turns, bringing him up-to-date.

"A few things stand out. If James's story is true, and he was so drunk he knocked over that table, why didn't Helen hear it?" Rob asked.

"Maybe she was a sound sleeper," Patty said.

Rob stood, walked to the table, and pushed it over. There was a loud bang that echoed in the large room. The girls ran from the other side of the house. Cindy said, "What was that?"

"You could hear that in the theater with the movie playing?" Rob asked.

"We're not deaf." Jenny shrugged and left with Cindy.

I sat up. "It was loud. That's a pretty heavy table."

"But she was older. Maybe her hearing wasn't good." Patrick walked to the table, and he and Rob righted it.

"Maybe she was already dead. Ugh. I don't even want to think about that." Patty shivered.

"I wish I knew what James was working on when I went to the library the other day. He stuffed those papers away like he was guilty of something. Too bad we made him move out. We might have been able to find out what was going on." I stood. "Wait a minute. He was pretty flustered when he left last night. Maybe he forgot to take them, and they're still here."

I walked down the hall to the library and checked the folders on the desk. The top ones contained receipts for James's expense reports and other work-related papers. The bottom one was a different story. I scanned the contents, hurried back to the living room, and slapped it on the coffee table. "Bingo."

Patrick's eyebrow rose. "What is it? He opened the folder. It was a spreadsheet with various people's names on the left-hand side, and columns with headers of 'Owed' and 'Repaid.' The balances in the first column overwhelmingly outweighed the sparse entries in the second.

I said, "James owed quite a few people a lot of money."

The doorbell rang. Patty rose to answer it. "It's late for someone to be calling."

Her voice echoed from the hall. "James. What are you doing here?"

"I realized I left a few things in the library I needed."

Patrick stood. "I better see what's going on."

"I'm missing a folder. Did you take it?" James's voice rose.

"We have it in the living room," Patrick answered.

James stalked into the living room, grabbed the folder, and glowered at me. "This is mine. Why would you take it?"

Rob leaped up so that he was between James and me.

Patrick walked to James's side. "We know about your debts, James. It looks like things were bad."

James sank onto a chair. "It's not easy paying alimony, supporting three kids, and maintaining my lifestyle."

Patrick put a hand on James's shoulder. "What did you get yourself into?"

"Horses. I love the ponies. There's nothing quite like watching them come around that last turn, dirt flying, jockeys' colorful silks flapping in the breeze. It makes me feel alive." He sighed. "I used to win, you know. I was good at reading the horses. I knew which one was destined for greatness.

"I hit a bad patch. Nothing was going my way, so I turned to people who'd make me a small loan, then bigger ones. Just until I hit it big again. I knew my luck would turn. I just didn't know how long it would take. This has been my longest dry spell." He looked up and smiled. "But Helen's passing means I can get out from under this debt. It also means I can play the ponies whenever I want.

"I'm going to use her money to make more money, you'll see."

* * *

"How can someone believe they can beat the odds consistently? Especially when they've lost before. I can't believe how much he owed those people. I wouldn't be able to sleep at night if I was in that much debt." I yawned.

Rob pulled me closer. "You're tired. It's time for you to go to sleep."

"I can't believe you're not tired. I've at least adjusted to this time zone." I snuggled closer to him. Patrick, Patty, and the girls had long since gone to bed.

"Night owl."

"I don't want to go to bed. I've missed you too much." I lifted my face for a kiss.

He obliged, and before long, we were prone on the sofa making up for lost time. I pushed away from him. "We need to stop."

"I know." He laughed. "One of these days—"

"Can't wait." I kissed his nose. "But for now, this young woman needs her beauty sleep."

Rob stood and held out his hand. I took it, and he pulled me to my feet. We trod up the stairs, and I gave him one last kiss at his door. "Love you."

"I love you too. Lock your door."

I gave a low chuckle. "Against you?"

"That too." He gave me one last hug and shut his door.

I meandered down the hall to my room, started to lock the door, and then stopped myself. Since James moved out, there wasn't anyone to lock out. Except Rob. I smiled as I brushed my teeth and changed into my nightgown. A few minutes later, I was under the covers and fast asleep.

A chair scraped across the floor, and my eyes flew open. Matilda sat near the bed. I scrabbled away. "What are you doing? What time is it?"

"I needed to talk to you."

I flipped on the light. "It's five o'clock."

"It's important." She leaned closer.

I scooted further away. "Why me? You work for Patrick and Patty. Shouldn't you be talking to them?"

"You helped me when I needed it most. I knew you'd listen, and I have to tell someone. I just know the police are going to find out, and then they'll arrest me."

I groaned and rubbed my eyes. "What did you want to talk about?"

"I'm worried. No one knows this, but I came in early that day."

"What day?"

She stood, went to the dresser, and grabbed a mug she must have brought with her. "Here. You like a bit of cream in yours, right? I think you need to wake up a bit."

I took the steaming mug, blew on it, and gave a careful sip. "Mm. Thanks. Are you saying you came in early the day Helen was killed?"

She shook her head. "Helen was so excited about Patrick that she called me when she got home from the restaurant that evening. She decided she would call him in the morning for a special brunch. She wanted me to make brioche French toast. It takes at least four hours to make the brioche, then it needs to soak, and finally, it needs to be baked. I was tired, but what could I say. I told her I'd come in early.

"My nephew had borrowed my car, so I called an Uber. I wanted to make a lemon-lime curd to go with the French toast, so to save time, I had him leave me at the back of the property, and I gathered lemons and limes as I walked toward the house. I let myself in by the kitchen and got to work."

"I thought your nephew was an attorney."

"That's Gail's son. This one's Sally's."

I plumped a pillow and put it behind my head. "What time did you get here?"

"Three-thirty. I barely had any sleep." She yawned. "I made the dough and put it in the proofing oven. Then I set the table in the dining room. I put one of the plates down, and it clanked. My head automatically turned toward the living room. I was worried I had woken someone. The table near the garage was overturned, and the vase that usually topped it was smashed on the ground. Nothing else was disturbed. I was still half asleep, so I righted the table and swept up the mess.

"The timer rang, and I went back to the kitchen and punched down the dough. As I shaped the bread, I got a bad feeling. Who would have overturned the table? Had there a struggle? What if someone was hurt? So I put the dough back in the oven and ran upstairs. I came to James's room first. He was snoring so loud I thought he'd take the roof off. Then I tiptoed to Helen's room. I put my head next to the door. I couldn't hear anything, so I pushed the door open a tad and peered in. A pillow was in the middle of the floor, I crept to her bed, flipped on the light, and there she was, dead.

"I almost screamed. I rushed out the door, shut it, and ran back down to the kitchen. I picked up the phone to call the police, and then put it down as if I'd been burned—how could I call the police? James was sound asleep, and I was in the house earlier than usual. They'd think I killed her because of the money. I threw out the dough, put the dirty bowl and utensils in the dishwasher, called Uber, and met them back behind the house.

"I returned home and waited near the front window. I kept thinking the police would pull up in front of the house at any minute. My nephew returned the car at five after he got off shift, and I left at five-thirty to return to Helen's at my normal time. I felt bad letting Louisa discover her body, but there would have been no reason for me to be upstairs. She delivered the coffee to the rooms, not me."

Halfway through Matilda's recitation, I had grabbed a pad and pen from the side table. I scribbled as she spoke. When she droned to a stop, my eyes lifted. "Did you tell your lawyer all this?"

"Of course not. I didn't tell anyone." She wrung her hands. "I'm worried the police will find out and think I killed her because I didn't tell them."

"That's a valid concern. I'd be surprised if they aren't scouring Helen's phone records right now. They're going to see she called, and they're going to want to know why you kept that to yourself."

"What should I do?"

"It will be far worse for you if the police come to your door. I suggest you call your lawyer and talk to him. I'm sure he'll want to go with you to come clean."

Matilda stood. "But what about breakfast? I can't leave now."

"I'll tell Patrick and Patty. You need to worry about you right now."

She nodded. The door shut, and I leaped out of bed to lock it. I was never going to leave my door open again in this house. I shuddered as I pulled the covers up over my shoulders. Not comfortable, I turned on my side. A faint yellow glow peaked from under the shutters. It would be dawn soon. There was no way I was going to be able to go back to sleep.

I took a quick shower, donned shorts and a t-shirt, and made my way downstairs. I pushed open the door to the kitchen. I was alone, but a carafe of coffee beckoned. I poured a cup and opened the refrigerator to get cream. There was Italian sausage on the top shelf, plus a dozen eggs. I checked the freezer; it had all the ingredients needed for an egg bake.

I stirred cream in my coffee and gathered everything I needed. Intent on browning sausage, I jumped when Rob kissed my neck. "You scared me!"

"I'm surprised to see you up so early."

"Coffee's over there." I pointed with the spatula.

He poured a cup. "Where's the chef?"

"Grab a baking pan, would you? I think they're in that cupboard there."

He held up two that were different sizes.

"Left hand."

He put it next to me on the counter. I layered the sausage, spinach, and hash browns in the pan, then whisked eggs and cream, poured them over the concoction, and topped it with cheddar cheese. "Let me put this in the oven, and then we'll talk."

"That looks delicious. How long does it take?"

"An hour." I put it on a rack, closed the oven, and set a timer.

He sat and pulled me onto his lap. "Now, why are you up so early?"

CHAPTER 26

Patrick

I woke early and couldn't get back to sleep. James was a gambler. Could I trust anything that he said? I put another pillow behind me and shifted higher in the bed. Patty's face looked so peaceful, and I couldn't bear to wake her. I lifted my book and then put it down again. I wasn't going to be able to concentrate. I walked into the bathroom, eased the door shut, and turned on the shower. The water played over my back as I rolled my shoulders, trying to release the tension. Finished, I dried off, put on shorts and a t-shirt, and eased the door open. Patty was awake.

"Did I wake you? I tried to be quiet." I kissed the top of her head.

"That's probably what woke me. I'm not used to the quiet."

I sank next to her on the bed. "I can't stop thinking about James. He lies repeatedly. How can I trust him? And, what if he didn't do it? How will he ever forgive me for kicking him out of the house? What if I finally found a family member, and he never speaks to me again?"

"What if you find out your family member killed your mother?"

"I don't know if I could stand it."

* * *

I trudged down the stairs and walked into the kitchen. "Matilda—"

Merry was pulling a pan from the oven, and Rob sat atop a stool at the island.

"Matilda's meeting with her lawyer, and I couldn't sleep."

"Neither could I. I'm still freaked out about James." I walked to the pan. The cheese was brown and bubbling. "What's this?"

"An egg bake. It needs to sit for a while before I cut it. Coffee's on the counter."

"Do you want to tell me why Matilda's with her lawyer?" I filled a mug.

Merry counted plates and set them down in front of Rob. "Would you mind setting the table? Silverware's in this drawer."

"Happy to," he said, as he picked them up and walked into the dining room.

"Matilda visited me early this morning."

"In your room?"

"Is Patty up? I already told Rob the story, and I'd rather not have to do this two more times." Merry retrieved orange juice from the refrigerator and handed it to me. "Please put this on the table."

Patty walked through the door. "Why are you cooking?"

Merry groaned. "Let's talk about this now, before the girls come down."

Patty, Rob, and I sat at the island. Merry leaned against the back counter and told us what happened.

"She was here that night?" My mouth dropped.

"Not night, but early in the morning." Merry clarified.

"Same thing," Patty interjected.

"She does kind of back up James's story."

My head tilted.

"The table. Matilda said it was overturned and that a vase had been smashed."

Rob said, "That table was pretty heavy for her to pick up."

I nodded. "I can't believe she discovered my mother's body and didn't alert anyone. What kind of person does that?"

"Someone who might be guilty," Patty said.

The door swung open. "Something smells good," Cindy said.

Merry jumped up. "Be out in a second, pour yourselves juice."

"To be continued." Rob held the door as Merry walked through with breakfast.

✳ ✳ ✳

Merry, Jenny, and Cindy took Rob to the Heard Museum. Patty and I decided to take the day off and relax by the pool. I arranged the umbrella over the chairs, and she came out with a large pitcher of ice water. She smiled as she poured it into two large glasses. "You know, this would almost be fun if everything else weren't going on. Here we are, alone, by this lovely pool with a whole day ahead of us."

My phone rang, and I picked it up. "Hello, Katie, what's going on?"

"Would you mind if I came over in about an hour?"

"What's up?"

"I want to talk about my inheritance. And the theater."

I pressed the speaker button and sprayed my arm with sunscreen. "Do you need James too? He moved to a hotel."

"Why would he do that?"

"Long story. If you want him to be here, you'll need to call him on his cell to arrange it."

"See you in an hour."

Patty finished spraying her legs. "Katie's coming over?"

"Something about her inheritance. She can talk to us here. I'm not moving."

"Maybe I should get things ready; they might like a snack." Patty sat up.

I put my arm out. "Water's fine. If they want more than that, they can get it themselves."

I must have dozed because it seemed like just a few minutes passed before the doorbell rang. Patty pulled on her cover-up, and I answered the door. James and Katie stood in the entryway. I extended my hand. "We're out by the pool."

Patty had refilled the ice water and gotten two more glasses. "Water?"

Katie and James nodded and sat at the table.

Katie said, "I'm sorry to bother you, but I wanted to talk about my inheritance."

"Didn't it come through? I could call Scott and find out how long it's going to take," I said.

She shook her head. "That's not it. The lawyer sent my check. The problem is that it's not enough."

James's head tilted. "Not enough? She left you a hundred thou. You can't have spent it already."

"It's not for me. It's for the theater. Gerard said he met with Patrick and Patty the other day. Have you given a donation any more thought? It's such a good cause." She leaned forward, hands clasped.

"It is. But you have to accept the fact this is all new to us. James," I pointed to him, "and I won't be receiving our money for a while yet. It's still working its way through. Plus, Patty and I aren't sure we are going to keep the house. You've been working on plans for the theater renovation for quite some time. What's the rush now?"

She shuffled her feet under the table, and her knuckles shone white from the pressure she was putting on the water glass. "I know this is sudden, but I thought Helen and I were pretty far along with our discussions."

Patty put her hand on Katie's arm. "And?"

Katie pulled away. "So I signed a contract. The construction is due to begin in two weeks, and I have to come up with a million dollars by then."

My mouth dropped. "A million dollars?"

"Fundraising has been going well, but it's been a lot of smaller donations. I need a big score if I'm going to meet the deadline." She sat back, shoulders slumped. Then she shot up. "James, you might be able to co-sign for a loan with me. They'll take your inheritance into account. You'll get what—twenty million? That might work."

James cleared his throat. "My credit isn't exactly what you might call stellar. I have odds and ends I need to clear up myself."

Her head swiveled toward me. "What about you?"

"You heard the lawyer. My inheritance is a million dollars."

"Which is exactly what we need."

"No. I'm sorry, but the answer is no. I can't help you."

"It's not like you knew her. You swooped in and practically stole her money." She stormed from the house.

Patty chewed on an ice cube. "That was a bit much, expecting us to give her our whole inheritance, plus you were Helen's son; it's not like you were no relation."

"Don't be offended by Katie. I admire her spunk. You know the old saying, 'If you don't ask you don't get.'" James stood. "I'll see myself out, bro."

Patty and I moved back to the lounge chairs, and she held my hand. "Did Katie upset you? I'm sure she didn't mean it. She was just panicking."

"That's a first."

"What?"

"You defending Katie." He kissed my hand.

I chuckled. "I guess I was."

"Let's try to enjoy the rest of the day."

* * *

"So, Katie was so sure Helen was going to give her the money that she signed an agreement?" Merry sipped her cabernet. "I'm surprised the builder didn't ask to see any paperwork from the bank before committing to the work."

"Huh. That is odd. Maybe Katie was planning on guilting Helen into it. Kind of what she tried to do with Patrick." Patty rubbed my shoulder.

"If she had so much money, wouldn't Helen have had an accountant?" Rob sat down next to me.

I nodded. "You're right; she would have."

Rob shrugged. "Maybe you should check with Helen's accountant to see if she was talking about transferring money or getting some kind of construction loan to fund the restoration."

Merry put her glass down on the table. "That's a good idea. Patrick, do you know who her accountant was?"

I said, "His number's probably in her address book. If I can't find it there, I could give her lawyer a call. He would know who it was."

Three pairs of eyes stared at me.

"Oh. You want me to look now."

Patty made a shooing motion with her hand.

Merry stood. "I'll help. It's probably in the credenza behind her desk. I've looked through the desk drawers already for paper and pens, and I would have seen it then."

Merry and I walked to Helen's office. I said, "You take the right; I'll take the left. One of these days I'm going to have to go through everything."

The address book was in the second drawer Merry opened. She said, "Eureka," and handed it to me.

I flipped through. "Here she is. Acton Accounting, Sheila Banning. It has a cell phone number for her. Read it to me, please." I handed the book to Merry. She told me the number as I punched it in my phone.

"Sheila Banning."

"Hello, Ms. Banning, this is Patrick Twilliger."

"Patrick—oh yes, Helen's son. I met you at her memorial service. Call me, Sheila."

"I'm afraid I met so many people that day—"

"No worries. What can I do for you?"

"Katie Glass stopped by today to discuss the Scottsdale Revival Theater."

Sheila groaned. "Oh, no. Helen told me she would drone on about it."

"So, Helen wasn't interested in funding the renovation."

Merry's mouth dropped. "What did she say?"

"Shhh."

"What?"

"Not you, Sheila. Please continue," I said.

"Helen liked Katie. She admired her, coming from nothing and making something of her life. She also liked the theater. But it wasn't her main interest, and she didn't want to invest all of her charitable monies into that one venture. To make up for it, and to support Katie, she'd hold fundraisers at her house."

"Why didn't she tell Katie she wasn't interested?"

Sheila coughed. "Have you ever told a good friend bad news, one whom you didn't want to disappoint?"

"Of course."

"Well—Helen didn't like to say 'no' to people."

My shoulders tensed. "Thanks for letting me know."

"I wanted to give you time to process Helen's death, but you, James, and I should get together in the next few weeks to go over some things. We can do it over the phone, if you're going back home."

"I'll give you a call when things are a bit more settled." I hung up.

Merry leaned toward me. "What did she say?"

"Let's find Patty and Rob." I walked out of the library, and Merry followed.

Patty was in the kitchen loading the dishwasher, and Rob sat at the island. Patty said, "Living in the lap of luxury, I had forgotten about such mundane tasks."

I motioned for her to move to the other side of the dishwasher and began to rinse dishes and hand them to her. Merry sat next to Rob.

Patty asked, "What happened?"

"Bottom-line, Helen strung Katie along. She never had any intention of investing in the theater." I handed her another dish.

"That sounds like kind of a harsh assessment." Patty put the plate in the dishwasher and reached for the pan I held out.

"The accountant—Sheila—didn't put it like that, she said Helen didn't like to say 'no' to people, and Katie wasn't intuitive enough to pick up on her clues."

Merry cleared her throat. "I wonder if she ever spoke to her lawyer about this."

"Only one way to tell." I lifted my phone and pressed Scott's number. "Sorry to bother you after hours. I was wondering if Helen ever spoke of leaving a bequest to benefit the Scottsdale Revival Theater.

"She did not."

"How about increasing the amount she was leaving to Katie?"

"She mentioned that one or two years ago, but then decided against it."

"Thanks for your time." I put the phone down.

Rob said, "Well?"

"Pretty much the same story as the accountant."

✳ ✳ ✳

The next morning found me on the phone with my boss explaining yet again why I was unable to leave. Patty hugged me after I put the phone down. "We'll get through this."

"What about your clients? Your interior design career was just taking back off."

She kissed my nose. "I'm talented. I'm helping my current customers remotely, and I'll get new ones when I get back. You're a good salesman. Your boss isn't going to drop you."

I sank onto a chair. "I hope not."

My phone rang. "Hello, Scott. What's up?"

"I have news for you. I heard from Katie's lawyer this morning. She's contesting the will. She believes you exerted undue influence on Helen and got her to change her will."

"What?"

"It's a frivolous suit. Helen hadn't changed her will in four years. I'll get it dismissed, but it may take a while. James is next on my call list." He hung up.

CHAPTER 27

Merry

"Can you imagine that? She's contesting the will—the nerve. Helen's will divided her property the way she wanted it. That woman's a gold digger." Patty flicked on the turn signal to pull into the grocery store parking lot.

"She's also a woman who's in trouble." I pointed. "There's a spot. Next to the blue car."

"I can't believe you're taking her side." Patty put the car in park.

"Never. You know I'll always be on your side. I'm just saying she may be getting desperate."

"Enough to do something?" Patty's eyes widened.

"Perhaps." I opened the door and stood. "Though I don't know what she'd gain from coming after any of us. It's not like she's a beneficiary of any of our wills."

Patty shivered as she wheeled the grocery cart. "I guess that makes me feel better."

I checked celery, carrots, and mushrooms off the list as I loaded the cart. Patty picked up a few avocados and limes. "Let's make guacamole."

"A pound of the chicken, sliced thin, please." I waited by the deli.

Katie loomed behind Patty. "Did you hear from your attorney?"

Patty jumped. "What are you doing here? Did you follow us?"

"Don't be silly." She gestured to her cart. "Grocery shopping, just like you."

"Patrick heard from his attorney. I don't know what you're hoping to accomplish."

"I just want what's mine. Helen promised me that money." Her voice rose.

The deli clerk said, "Here's your chicken."

I had my hand out, but Patty grabbed it from him and said, "Helen was humoring you; she was never going to give you that money."

"She was too. She believed in my vision."

"She believed in you, not the theater," I said gently.

"You're lying." Katie shoved her full cart straight at Patty, and Patty went down like a sack of potatoes. Katie stalked away through the automatic doors.

The deli clerk sprinted around the corner, and he and I moved the cart away from Patty. He said, "Are you all right, Ma'am?"

She brushed hair from her face. "I think I'm okay."

The clerk and I each grabbed an arm and lifted her to her feet. She rubbed her shin. "That's going to leave a bruise."

"Do you want me to call the police? I can't believe she did that." The clerk shook his head.

"I'm okay. But I think we'll cut this shopping trip short." Patty dusted off her shorts and inspected her right elbow. "Ow. I think I landed on this one."

"Maybe I should take you to the hospital," I said.

"I'm fine. I'll wait in the car."

"I'll be right there."

"Do you need help to the car?" The clerk asked Patty.

"Thank you for your help; I'll be fine." She limped out the door.

I hurried through checkout. Just before I exited, the deli clerk handed me two baggies filled with ice and said, "I hope she feels better."

Patty was reclining in the passenger seat, and Katie was standing by her door. "I'm just so sorry. I don't know what came over me. You said Helen never intended to give me the money, and I saw red. You have to believe I've never done anything like that before."

I said, "Excuse me," handed Patty the bags of ice, and began loading the trunk.

"I didn't mean to do that. You have to believe me."

"But you did." I glared at Katie as I slammed the trunk shut, and then got in the driver's side door.

"We've all done stupid things." Patty handed me the keys.

"Not assault." I started the car.

"Katie, I believe you." Patty rolled up the window and closed her eyes. I drove away, and Katie stood there, looking like a lost child.

"Thanks for the ice. My shin's throbbing in time with my elbow." Patty gritted her teeth.

"Hospital? Or home?"

"Home. The ice is helping a lot, and I don't think anything's broken."

When we got near, I called Patrick's phone on speaker. "We're going to need help."

He said, "I'll send the girls out."

"I need you or Rob," Patty protested.

"I thought you were just getting a few things at the store."

"We're pulling in now. Meet us in the garage."

I pressed the button, and the door rose. I parked the car. "I can see why you like this car."

Patrick came out of the house. "Pop the trunk."

"Patty's hurt. Help her out. I'll get the groceries." I pointed toward the passenger door.

"What happened?" He rushed to the door and opened it. "Were you in a car accident?"

"You had an accident?" Rob walked into the garage and looked me up and down. "Are you okay?"

"I'm fine. Help Patrick with Patty."

Patty handed Patrick the ice packs, and he passed them to Rob.

"I just got a little banged up." She swiveled her legs from the car and reached her left hand toward Patrick. "Slowly."

Patrick took her hand and pulled gently. Rob tried to help by grasping her right elbow, and she yelped, "Not that arm!"

He dropped it. "Sorry."

"You didn't know." Patty limped toward the door. "Take the groceries from Merry, Rob."

Patrick hovered. "What can I do?"

"Help me up the steps."

He shoved the door open, and half carried her up the two steps into the living room. She wobbled to one of the sofas and collapsed as Rob brought in the groceries, and I the baggies of ice. Patrick stood over Patty. "What happened? Should you go to the emergency room?"

I handed the ice to Patty. She put one on her elbow, kicked off her shoes, put her legs on the couch, and balanced the other on her shin. "That feels better."

I sat on the facing sofa. "Katie ran into Patty with her shopping cart."

Patrick's eyebrow rose. "What?"

Patty motioned to the seat next to her. "Sit down. Katie got upset when I told her Helen had no intention of giving her the money. In retrospect, it might not have been the smartest thing to do."

Patrick sat. "Should we call the police? That's assault!"

"She apologized. She said she just lashed out." Patty lifted the ice from her leg. It was turning a lovely blue-green color.

"Are you sure you don't need to go to the hospital?" Patrick kissed her forehead.

"I've had enough excitement for one day."

* * *

Patty was lying on the couch, one pillow propping up her leg, and another, her arm, leafing through a magazine. I was working on my laptop. The door opened, and Matilda walked in. "I thought we might have Cornish game hens with a mushroom sauce for dinner."

Patty's eyes widened. "Matilda, what are you doing here?"

"My nephew got them to release me. What happened to you?"

"It's a long story. Cornish hens sound delicious."

I nodded. "They sound great."

She turned on her heel and walked back into the kitchen.

Patty waved her hand, beckoning me closer and whispered, "I can't believe Matilda's back."

"It is awkward."

"What should I do?"

Matilda walked back into the living room with a large pitcher of pink lemonade. "I thought you might like something refreshing." Matilda plunked iced into both glasses, filled them, and handed them to us. "Enjoy."

She left the pitcher on a tray and returned to the kitchen.

The floral scent of lemons pervaded the room. Patty studied the glass.

"I should go back to work. Isn't it time for you to do more ice?" Not waiting for an answer, I strode to the kitchen and walked through the swinging door.

Matilda was chopping mushrooms with a vengeance and looked up as I came in. I said, "Just getting ice for Patty."

She put the blade down. "I need this job. Do you think you could talk to them?"

I gulped. "It's a troubling time for everyone. Hopefully, we'll get answers soon, and everything will get back to normal." I eased out the door and walked back to the living room.

Patrick came down the stairs. "How are you feeling?"

"A little sore," Patty grumbled.

I handed her the ice packs, lifted my laptop, and sat down.

"That lemonade looks good." He retrieved a glass and poured.

Patty said, "Matilda's back."

Patrick sat next to me. "Is it wise to have her here while she's still under investigation?"

"Who knows?" She shrugged. "The good news is none of us need to cook." She turned toward me. "What took you so long to get the ice?"

I sighed. "Matilda. It seems I've somehow become her confidant. She's worried you're going to turn her loose."

"Patrick and I are struggling with it."

"She knows. She wants to make it up to you. She says she needs this job."

"Ugh. Why does everything need to be so complicated?" Patty pointed to the girls outside by the pool. "Why can't we be like them and get to sunbathe without a care in the world?"

"I wouldn't want to be seventeen again. So many emotions. So much drama." I pulled a pillow onto my lap.

Patrick sipped lemonade. "Don't worry about it, Patty. We don't have to make a decision today."

"I know. It just seems that lately, we've been pushing out a lot of stuff we're going to have to deal with at some point in time."

* * *

As we were enjoying a pre-dinner cocktail, the doorbell rang. No one else moved, so Patrick stood. "I'll get it."

There were raised voices, and a minute or two later, Katie stood in the doorway, holding a cake carrier in front of her. "I bring a peace offering."

Rob and I jumped to our feet, and Patrick stood sentry, an arm's length distance from Katie, looking like he was ready to haul her off if

210

she made the slightest wrong move. He said, "Patty, let me know if you want her to leave."

"Does it hurt?" Katie nodded toward Patty's leg.

Patty asked, "What are you doing here? And, yes, it does, thanks to you."

"I made you a cake because I felt so bad about lashing out." Katie put the cake carrier on the coffee table. "It's vanilla with chocolate frosting."

Patty sat up, and the ice pack slipped from her leg. The blue and brown colors now had a tinge of yellow.

"That looks awful. I'm so sorry."

Katie looked like she was going to cry, and Patty said, "It's okay. I probably shouldn't have told you Helen was never going to give you the money."

"I thought a lot about it this afternoon. Sometimes I'm like a dog with a bone. I think the mere force of my convictions will make people as enthusiastic as me." She pushed the cake carrier closer to Patty. "I hope you'll accept this and my apology."

Patty lifted the cover. The cake had a chocolate mirror glaze and was decorated with small green and yellow flowers. "This is pretty. Does this mean you're not going to challenge the will?"

"I'm sorry for pushing the cart. Not for contesting. I hope you enjoy the cake." She walked out of the room, and Patrick followed her. The door slammed, and a lock clicked into place.

Patty and I exchanged glances. Patty said, "We're not eating this cake."

"Agreed. Can't be too safe."

Patrick returned. "We're not going to eat it?"

"Nope."

"Not even a little slice?" Rob leaned over the cake.

I snapped the carrier lid on and strode to the kitchen, where Matilda was emptying the trash. I slid the cake toward her. You can put this in there too."

She gave me a strange look. "You want to throw the whole thing out?"

"Just the cake, and then in a few days, please call Katie to pick up the carrier."

"Okay."

I returned to the living room and lifted my drink. "All better."

Patrick sat next to Patty. "But it looked so good."

Patty said, "We're eating enough. I'm sure Matilda has another fabulous dessert planned for tonight."

* * *

The next morning, I wandered into the kitchen as Matilda ladled batter into a waffle iron. It sizzled, and cinnamon wafted into the air. She flipped the iron and looked up. "That cake Katie made was great. It had five layers, alternating pastry cream, and a raspberry filling. The friends I invited for a late supper loved it."

"I thought you were going to throw it out."

"Seemed like such a waste."

I coughed as I filled my mug. "I'm glad you enjoyed it." As I exited the kitchen, I whispered under my breath, "and lived."

Patty limped into the dining room, and I grabbed her arm. "Matilda ate the cake."

"Is she dead?"

"If she were dead, how would I know she ate it? That's silly."

Rob traipsed down the stairs, suitcase in hand. He joined us. "I can't believe I have to leave today."

I stood and kissed him. "Me, either."

"Breakfast." Matilda came in with a platter. "Cinnamon waffles with strawberry syrup. There's more coming, so you can get started."

"I'm going to miss this great service." Rob sat and put a napkin on his lap.

I texted the girls and Patrick that breakfast was ready, then turned to Rob. "What time do you get in?"

"Ten, if everything runs smoothly." He rapped on the table.

I selected a waffle from the platter and passed it to Patty. She put one on her plate and added butter and sugar. She said, "Better start eating; you'll need to leave soon."

Cindy and Jenny ran down the stairs, and Jenny grabbed the pitcher of juice from the sideboard. "I can't believe you're leaving already, Mr. Jenson."

"I need to get back. Work—a lot of things are happening this weekend, and I'm taking the boys to another baseball game tomorrow night."

Patty said, "I can't thank you enough for all you're doing for Patrick and me. And my parents! They're so relieved you're coming back."

"It's fun for me. Kids have so much energy. They're great." Rob stared at me.

Jenny looked straight down, speared a waffle, and busied herself with the butter and syrup. Then she pushed the waffle around the plate. I gave her a quick glance.

Patty sighed. "I miss them."

My phone buzzed. "Time to go."

"I'll see you when you get back." Rob gave Jenny a quick hug and waved to Patty and Cindy. He lifted his suitcase, and he and I left.

CHAPTER 28

Merry

Rob pulled me close and hugged me. "I can't believe I'm leaving you again. Promise me you'll be careful, and you'll lock your door at night."

"I promise." I kissed him and moaned, "You taste so good."

"Have you given any more thought to our discussion on kids?"

"I have. We'll talk about it when I get back."

He gave me a deeper kiss.

I gasped. "A little public in here for that."

He grinned and stepped into the security line.

I blew him one last kiss and waved. Grinning, I made my way back to the car. As I slid into the driver's seat, I pulled out my phone and tapped in "cupcakes near me." Three shops popped up. One was rated five stars by over three hundred people. That was my kind of shop. I turned on the radio, put the car in gear, and pressed the gas.

There was a vacant spot in front, so I took it. "Kittie's Cupcakes." *My two favorite things: cats and cupcakes.* I walked into the shop, and a bell rang. The line was about five deep, so I examined the selections. The curved, glass-front display showcased beautifully decorated cupcakes with a small sign that identified the type. Finally, I approached the counter and ordered. "I'd like twelve, please. Four each of the chocolate mint crunch, the chocolate ganache, and the vanilla."

Then I texted Patty: "Up for a ride? Be out front in ten."

"Sure."

I pulled up in front of the house, and Patty came out. She hopped in the car. "Where are we going? And what is that smell?"

I pointed to the pink boxes in the back. "We're going to the police station, and we're bringing gifts to loosen their tongues. We're going to find out where they are with this investigation because I need to go home."

She tried to edge the box open. "They smell divine."

I smacked her hand. "You can see them when we get there."

"Had an interesting conversation with Jenny after you left for the airport."

"And?"

"She was concerned about you getting pregnant, given your advanced age and all." Patty smiled.

"I'm not that old."

"Geriatric pregnancy. Just saying."

I flipped on the turn signal, drove into the lot, and parked. I sighed. "I don't know what to do."

Patty got out of the car. "I was surprised you told her about it if you haven't decided yet."

I handed her one box and picked up the other. "I didn't intend to. She caught me modeling a pillow."

"What?"

"I was trying to remember what it felt like. It's been seventeen years." I groaned and pushed the door to the station open with my hip. "Let's talk about this later."

I made my way to the desk sergeant. "Are either Detective Schwartz or Lieutenant Muniz in?"

"You're in luck, lady. Which one did you want to see?"

"I guess Lieutenant Muniz."

"Names?"

We told him.

He lifted the phone and pressed a button. "Two ladies to see you. A Ms. March and Ms. Twilliger."

"He'll be down shortly." He pointed with a pencil. "You can take a seat there if you like."

I eyed the uncomfortable wooden bench with unidentified stains. "That's okay; we'll stand."

We moved away from the desk. A few minutes later, the door opened, and Lieutenant Muniz walked toward us. "What can I do for you, ladies?"

Patty moved forward. "We wanted to get an update on the case. My husband's employer is getting antsy for him to come back."

I held out one of the boxes. "We drove by the cutest shop, and I thought you would like these cupcakes."

He took them from me. "These look like they're from Kittie's."

Patty smiled and handed him her box. "They are."

He led us back to his office and set them on his desk. Then he opened a drawer and used scissors to cut the ribbon that held them shut. The lid rose.

Patty gasped. "Those are beautiful. They're like little pieces of art."

He opened the other box and lifted a cupcake decorated with three small chocolate squares. "This is my favorite. I love crunchies."

Detective Schwartz strolled in and nodded to us. "There's a rumor Kittie's Cupcakes are on the premises."

The lieutenant extended the box. "Take one."

He took a chocolate ganache.

"Would you like one?" The lieutenant turned toward Patty and me.

"We had a big breakfast." I patted my stomach. "We're good. As I mentioned, we wanted to get an update on the case."

"It's progressing." The lieutenant licked chocolate from his fingers and then wiped them with a napkin. He reached his hand toward another mint crunchy.

I pulled the box toward me and lowered the lid.

He sat back. "That's not fair."

I shrugged.

"Okay. We'll tell you a few things."

I pushed the box back toward him, and he moved it out of my reach.

Detective Schwartz pulled his notebook from his pocket and flipped through. "Did you know your new brother-in-law has a gambling problem?"

Patty nodded.

"Oh." He flipped further back. "Matilda was at the house early the morning Helen was killed."

"Know that." I sat back in my chair.

His eyebrow rose. "Katie admitted she went to the house that night."

"Yep. Don't you have anything new?"

The lieutenant finished his second cupcake. "This isn't the first time James has been in trouble. Last year, he was arrested in Idaho for threatening a man with a knife. The guy ended up not pressing charges, and James's fancy lawyer convinced the prosecutor they didn't have a good enough case. They dropped the charges, but it means he's got a history of violence."

Patty's mouth dropped.

The lieutenant balled up the cupcake wrappers and tossed them into the trash like it was a basketball net. He smirked. "Well, if there isn't anything else?"

I rose. "Enjoy the cupcakes."

✳ ✳ ✳

James sat on one of the sofas, and Patty, Patrick, and I sat on the other. James drummed his fingers on the couch arm. "This feels like an inquisition."

"Maybe it is." Patrick selected an apple, tossed it up, and caught it. He repeated the action. "Merry and Patty spoke with the police this morning. They said you attacked someone with a knife in Idaho."

James stood. "Anyone want a drink? If this is the way the evening's going to go, I think I'll need one."

"Beer for me." Patrick raised his hand.

Patty shook her head, and I raised my water glass.

James popped the tabs on two cans and handed one to Patrick. Then he sank onto the sofa. He took a swig and ran his fingers through his hair. "It was nothing. Okay?"

We waited.

"I was at this bar near my house, having a few and enjoying a steak dinner. Then this guy comes in with his girlfriend. She was a knockout. Long curly flaming-red hair—" He looked at me "—kinda like yours, but longer."

I rolled my eyes.

"Anyway, she was a looker. I've always had a thing for redheads. They sit at the bar, and two minutes later, they're fighting. Something about his friend and the amount of attention she's been paying him. I was trying not to listen, but I was three seats down, and there wasn't much else going on. So she says, 'if he didn't quit being so jealous she'd leave him.' At that, he roars and stands over her. He says, 'I'd kill you first,' and pulls back his arm. I leaped up, and I swear I didn't realize I still had the steak knife in my hand, and, before I knew it, I was two inches from him, screaming he better leave her alone.

"The owner called the cops, and they arrested me for threatening him with a knife. Luckily the girlfriend talked him into dropping the charges, and my lawyer talked to the district attorney. Otherwise, I would have been in big trouble."

Patrick relaxed his grip on the beer can. "When Patty told me about it, I was worried it was because of your gambling debts. That one of the people you owed came after you, and things went south."

"Bro, I swear to you, it went down exactly like I said." James's hand unclenched the sofa cushion.

"Is there anything else we should know before the police tell us? Any other assaults they're going to find out about?" I crossed my legs.

"Nothing."

"No restraining orders, nothing like that?"

James shook his head. "Clean as a whistle."

I looked at Patty, "Any other questions?"

She leaned forward. "Is there anything you're holding back?"

"No. And, if there aren't any further questions, I have one for you."

"Fire away." Patrick sipped his beer.

"What are we going to do about Katie contesting the will?"

"Scott said it's a nuisance suit. It should be resolved soon."

"I need the money. My lenders are getting antsy and, even though I've shown them the paperwork, they don't quite trust me. If she doesn't back off, or if she leaks the fact that she is contesting to the newspapers, things are going to get dicier than they already are." James stood, crushed the beer can, and tossed it in the trash. The front door shut behind him.

Patrick put his head in his hands. "I wish this nightmare would end."

* * *

My phone rang early the next morning, and I lifted it to my ear. "Good morning, Rob. How was the plane ride?"

"Long and crowded. What did you do after I left?"

I told him.

"Hold on." There was muttering in the background. "I need to go in a minute; the town council is about to start debating what to do in mid-summer when the flowers in the square begin to brown."

I chuckled. "Serious business. I'll hang up after one more thing. Would you do me a favor?"

"Anything."

"Can you check out James's story? I'll text you the town and the name of the bar."

"No problem." He cleared his throat. "Don't forget, Drew's extradition came through. He'll be arraigned in New York today."

I groaned. "I hadn't forgotten. Love you."

"Love you too." He hung up.

I stretched and opened the blinds. Clouds were gathering, and it looked like it was going to rain. There was a knock at my door, I unlocked it, and Jenny walked in. I hopped back into bed, and Jenny joined me. I put my arm around her. "What's up?"

"I love you, Mom. I don't know what I'd do if you weren't around. If you want to have another baby, I guess it'd be okay."

"We've been through a lot." I squeezed her. "You and I will always have a special bond. No matter what happens, I will always love you."

"What am I going to call Mr. Jenson? If you two get married, it'll seem weird me calling him that."

"What would you like to call him?"

"I don't know." She chewed a fingernail. "I'm not going to call him Dad."

"He wouldn't expect that; he knows you have a father you love." I paused. "Speaking of which, your dad's arraignment is today."

She grimaced and then snuggled next to me. "I remembered."

I held out my hand. "Want to give me your phone?"

"One last text to Jacob." Her fingers flew. "Done." She handed me the phone. "Can I get it back later?"

"Whenever you want." I kissed her forehead. "Who knows, maybe everything's died down, and no one will care."

"Hopefully." She sat up. "What about an acronym for Mr. Jenson? BPM."

"What?" I pulled away so I could look her in the eye.

"Best Pancake Maker."

"Maybe you should think about this a bit more." I chuckled.

She leaped up and walked to the French doors. "It's raining. What are we going to do today?"

"Movie marathon?"

She pounced on the bed. "Great idea. Cindy and I will pick." She ran out the door.

I hopped in the shower, turned on the body jets, and closed my eyes. I hoped things would go well with the arraignment and that the trial date wouldn't be too far out. The spray massaged my back. *I'm going to miss this.* I toweled off, donned a robe, and pulled a shirt and shorts from the drawer. I was getting kind of tired of these clothes. *I should have brought more.*

Patty and I met by the stairs and walked down to breakfast. I touched her elbow. "Stop for a moment. What did you think about James's story?"

"I still don't know. Patrick and I talked about it till late last night. It could've happened like he said, but all of the discrepancies are starting to add up. I don't know what to believe. And what was that about Katie? He worries me. You don't think he'd do anything?" She rubbed the back of her neck. "All this stress is making my neck hurt."

"I asked Rob to look into the bar incident. It seems like he knows people everywhere. Plus, his reporter's nose doesn't hurt either."

"Thanks." She gave me a side hug. "I wonder what Matilda's made for breakfast this morning."

CHAPTER 29

Patrick

I was happy to hear the girls decided on a movie marathon after so much time in the sun. With negotiation, the consensus was "Harry Potter." Patty started the popcorn machine, and Matilda refilled the small fridge with sodas and waters. As she stacked them, she asked, "Hot dogs for lunch? I'll serve them on the table in the back."

"That's sounds great. Thanks." Merry took one of the sodas that didn't fit, popped the top, and reclined her seat. "I'm ready to go. Hit play."

We had just reached the part where Dobby got a sock from the evil wizard when my phone buzzed. I pulled it from my pocket and read a text from Katie: "Need help. James is threatening me for contesting the will and delaying his payout, and he may be violent. He says if I meet him at the Dobbins Lookout at four, he'll give me the first installment, but I don't trust him. Can you come?"

I texted back: "Not sure."

"I guess I could call the police so they could check it out, but I need the money."

I squirmed—I didn't want her to call the police—it would be another strike against my brother. Maybe James was going to pay her off. But how had he gotten enough money, even if it was an installment? If he was going to harm Katie, I needed to protect him from himself. My fingers flew. "I'll be there."

"Come alone. Or I will call the police."

Patty mouthed, "What's up?"

"Work." I put the phone back in my pocket. I didn't want to leave, and it felt weird not telling Patty what was going on. I shifted in the seat. If I told her, she and Merry would want to come, and that might screw things up for James. I sighed. It was better to hold off on involving them until I knew more.

The third movie had just ended, and Jenny was putting *Harry Potter and the Goblet of Fire* in the Blu-ray player. I stood. "Hate to duck out, but I have a few things I need to do. One of the auto dealers here has a new way of buffing dents to make cars look like new, and my boss wants me to check it out. I'll be back before dinner."

Patty kissed me goodbye. "Don't be too long."

"I won't. Love you."

She waved and turned back to the screen.

I input Dobbins Lookout into the GPS, and it plotted a route. As I followed the instructions, I ground my teeth. What was James up to? Why couldn't he just tell the truth? Had he killed my mother? I tried to relax my jaw, but it tensed up within seconds. It had been kind of fun having a brother. I didn't want to lose him.

The GPS alerted me that the turn was in four hundred feet. It looked like there was a hiking trail, but I opted for the winding road leading to the top. It was narrow, and I had a close call with a bicyclist who was coming down the mountain. It looked like people were packing up and leaving because another storm was coming in. I pulled into the parking lot just a few minutes before four and noted Katie's SUV parked by some kind of stone structure. I pulled in next to her and got out of the car. I didn't see James's rental, but Katie had her back to me near a bench overlooking a breathtaking view of Phoenix.

"Katie?"

She turned, hugging herself. "I'm glad you came. I've been so worried."

"Tell me what's been going on." I led her to the bench, and we sat.

Her eyes started to tear. "The phone calls started last night. Caller ID showed the hotel where you had been staying. I knew James had a room there, so I called his cell. It was awful. He screamed at me. He told me if I didn't back off on contesting the will, he'd get me. He threatened my dog. Who'd do that?"

"Then what happened?"

She coughed. "I have two bottles of water in my car. Mind getting them? It's not locked."

I jogged toward the car, lifted the bottles from the console, and returned. I handed her one.

She shook her head. "Switch bottles, I already drank from that one—see, the paper is torn."

I handed her the one I had. "What time is he supposed to be here?"

"Four." She glanced at her phone and frowned. "He's late."

I turned to scan the parking lot.

"Here's the text he sent." She scrolled through her phone and then handed it to me. The text from James read: "Have solution to both our problems; meet me at Dobbins Lookout at four."

"Well, he's not here yet, what do you think he meant?"

All of the muscles in her face looked taut. "I was hoping for money. I know I'm probably being silly." Her shoulders drooped, and she swigged more water.

My mouth was dry, so I unscrewed the lid of my bottle. "Huh, this was open."

"I always open them when I put them in the car. Have you ever tried opening one when you're driving?" She laughed and pantomimed struggling with the top.

I chuckled and then drained half the bottle. "What time is it now?"

"Four-twenty."

"Should we wait? I could call—" My body started feeling limp. "That's weird."

"What is?"

"Body feels strange." I laughed. "Is the city moving?"

"Might be. Let's get a little closer." She took my hand and led me toward the railing.

I staggered. "It's so beautiful. I could fly."

"Maybe you should try. Wait. I know what we should do. We should take a selfie."

"You come up with the best ideas." I laughed again. "Let's take a selfie. I'm going to take a selfie, selfies are fun, selfies are selfun."

She came back from her car with a selfie stick. "Let's use this. Oh, you know what would be better?"

I couldn't stop grinning. "What?"

"Climb up on the rail. You'll get a much better picture from there."

"Shouldn't we wait for James? I'd love a picture with my brother and me."

"We can do one with him later. Here, I'll steady you as you climb. Wait, where's your phone? We need to put it on the stick."

I patted my pockets and giggled. "Oops. No phone. My bad."

"We'll just use this one." She affixed a phone to the stick. "Okay, now just put your foot there—"

I climbed the two rungs and swayed. "Whew. Dizzy, need to sit."

"Not yet. Here, take this." She handed me the stick.

CHAPTER 30

Merry

The movie started, and I grabbed another container of popcorn for Patty and me to share. I tossed a few kernels in my mouth.

Cindy turned around. "Mom, shut off your phone, that vibrating is annoying."

Patty glanced at her phone. "Not mine."

I looked at mine. "Not me."

"Oh, I know what happened." Patty felt the edges of Patrick's seat and pulled out his phone. She glanced at the screen, climbed over my legs, and whispered, "I'll be right back."

I turned my attention back to the screen. A few minutes later, the door opened again, and Patty waved for me to come out. I walked out the door, and she shut it behind me.

I asked, "What's—"

"That was Patrick's boss. He didn't ask him to visit a dealership. I checked his texts—" She stiff-armed the phone to me, and I read the text from Katie.

"Oh no," I said.

"Got that right. Let's go."

I stuck my head into the theater room. "We need to go out for a few minutes. Something came up."

Jenny's hand appeared above the recliner with a dismissive wave.

We ran to the car and hopped in. Patty drove, while I typed in the address. Siri gave turn by turn directions, and it was a good thing there were no cops around as Patty probably would have been arrested for speeding. Patty's one hand rubbed her stomach, the other clenched the wheel. "Looks like it's going to storm."

I handed her antacids. "Chew these; they'll help."

She popped them into her mouth.

"Turn here!" I shouted.

The car fishtailed as she made the turn onto the road leading to the Lookout. I braced like a starfish, one hand on the console, the other in the strap, and both feet spread against the floor.

A car coming in the other direction nearly ran us off the narrow, winding road. Through gritted teeth, Patty said, "Slowing down." The steep drop-offs on either side made it a slog to get to the top of the mountain. I let out a breath I didn't know I'd been holding when we reached the top.

My phone rang. "It's Father Tom."

"You'll have to call him back."

I pointed to the far end of the fast emptying parking lot. "There."

Katie and Patrick were sitting on a park bench. My phone rang again. "I guess Father Tom really wants to talk to me."

A bicyclist came out of nowhere and shot in front of us, heading for the exit. Patty slammed on the brakes. "That was close." She slowed the car to a crawl.

All of a sudden, Patrick and Katie stood. Then it looked like Patrick was doing a jig. Katie walked back to her car, pulled out some kind of stick, and returned to him.

Patty asked, "What is he doing?"

I put my phone down. "I don't know, but he's getting awfully close to that railing."

Then Patrick started climbing, wobbling on the way up. Patty screamed and floored it. We reached their cars, and Patty barely stopped the one we were in before she flung herself out the door. I was behind her and grabbed the back of her shirt. "Careful. There's something wrong with him, and if you startle him, he may fall."

The blood drained from Patty's face. Fat raindrops fell as we crept closer, and Katie handed Patrick the stick. She said something about his phone, and then attached the one she had.

Patrick's face lifted, and he grinned. "Patty, come here. We're going to do selfies. Doesn't that sound great?"

Katie's head jerked around, and her mouth dropped.

Patty said, "Patrick, you need to come down. It's not safe."

"You're never any fun." He blew a raspberry.

Katie moved closer to Patrick, arms outstretched like she was going to shove him over the edge.

Patty ran toward her like a linebacker, shoulder down, and rammed Katie sideways, away from him. Katie flew a foot and went down hard on the dirt.

Patrick wobbled. I grabbed the bottom of his shirt and yanked him toward me. "Oh no, you don't."

His foot slipped from the rung, and he fell forward, arms bracing his fall as his body landed hard on top of me. He said, "Ow. What'd you go and do that for? That hurts. We were just trying to have fun."

Patty yelled, "Merry, are you okay?"

I lay there, trying to breathe. Finally, I gasped and rolled Patrick off of me. "Lost my breath for a moment. That hurt."

Patty scrabbled on top of Katie and sat on her, while Katie pummeled Patty's hips and squirmed like a slippery eel. Patty batted at her but was having trouble maintaining her position. Then Patty slapped her face.

Katie cried, "That hurt!"

"You were going to push my husband over the edge and make his four children lose their father." She called over her shoulder, "There's twine in Helen's trunk."

I ran to the car, popped the trunk, and grabbed the rope. Katie was bucking like a horse and grunting with the effort. I edged in and grabbed one of Katie's hands just as her other shot out, nailing my jaw. It was a tussle, but between the two of us, we were finally able to tie Katie's hands and feet.

Patty rushed to Patrick and sank by his side. "Are you all right?"

He was asleep, snoring loudly.

She shook his shoulder. He swatted at her hand and continued to snore. Patty glared at Katie. "What did you give him?"

"Why should I tell you?"

Patty made a fist and began pulling her arm back as she walked toward Katie. "I think you'd better. Don't forget; I have three boys."

"Just a Quaalude. Who knew he was going to react like that?" Katie laughed.

I looked over the railing—a sheer drop. I shivered. "What was the plan?"

"People fall taking selfies all the time. Idiots. I figured what's one more. The police probably wouldn't even have questioned it." She frowned. "Huh. The only problem was he forgot his phone. Who forgets their phone? Good thing I got a burner on my way here."

I called the police. After giving them the particulars, I pressed the phone to my shirt. "It's going to take them a while to get here, that road is terrible. I asked for an ambulance for Patrick, just in case."

"Thanks." Patty sank onto the bench and turned toward Katie. "I still don't understand. What would you get out of this?"

"A chance."

"A chance for what?" I sat next to Patty, one hand rubbing my jaw, the other my side.

"You two aren't the smartest aces in the deck, are you?"

Patty sighed. "We're not the ones tied up on the ground."

"My lips are sealed."

"Okay. Then I won't do anything about that small scorpion by your left hip."

"Like I'm going to believe that." Katie's eyes shifted and tracked the scorpion as it scurried toward her. She tried to wiggle away, but it seemed to have a homing beacon. She yelled, "Kill it. Kill it!"

"I might, but then again, you did just try to hurt my husband." Patty examined her nails. "Did you know it's the smaller scorpions that are more deadly?"

"I'll talk, I promise, just kill it."

Patty stood, walked over to the scorpion, and squished it. "Now, where were we? Oh yes, how does any of this make sense?"

"If Patrick died within twelve days, you wouldn't get the money, James would."

"How does that help you? Was James in on this?"

"Not yet. I thought if I killed Patrick, and James got the house and the additional money, he might toss me what I needed for the theater as a thank you."

Patty screeched, "You tried to kill Patrick on spec? You didn't even know James would give you the money?"

Katie shrugged. "It was a chance. It's all Helen's fault. When Patrick showed up, she was so excited. She called me that last night, nattering on, said he was all she dreamed he'd be and wasn't it so special they'd had this unexpected reunion, blah, blah, blah. And, then, she mentioned she was going to meet with her attorney to change her will the next day. I thought I knew what that meant. I was going to get the short end of the stick." She barked a laugh. "Who knew he was already in the will, and that she never intended to give me the money I thought she would.

"The house was dark, and when I rolled past the driveway, I saw James's car was gone. I relaxed a bit. Helen was home alone. I cruised by and parked my car out of sight of the cameras. Then, I snuck in the back, tiptoed up to her room, and pushed the door open. She was snoring softly, and a pillow had fallen next to the bed. It was a sign.

"I lifted it and covered her face. At first, I thought it was going to be easy, but then she began to fight. I had no idea how strong she was. I held it tighter and used more pressure. Eventually, her body relaxed, and I knew she was dead.

"When the lawyer read the will, I felt cheated. I still do. Who the heck is he—" She gestured with her bound hands toward Patrick "—to get the money. My money."

Sirens bloomed in the distance as a steady rain began to fall. Patty grabbed a blanket from the trunk and put it over Patrick. "It's going to get pretty wet, let's wait in the car."

"What about me?" Katie yelled after us.

"Who cares?" Patty ducked into the car as the rain came down in torrents. I eased onto the passenger seat and groaned. Patty turned toward me. "Are you sure you're okay?"

"Maybe not." I reclined my seat. "My side feels like it's on fire."

"We'll get the EMT to take a look at you too."

"You should probably call James to tell him what happened." I shut my eyes and tried to will away the pain.

✳ ✳ ✳

The ambulance took Patrick and me, and Patty followed in the car. Patrick slept on one hospital bed in the emergency room, and I occupied the other, holding an ice pack to my jaw.

The doctor said, "You have a cracked rib. That means no sports and no heavy lifting. If you feel any discomfort, stop what you're doing immediately."

"How long will it take to heal?"

"About six weeks. But it will take longer if you test it. So don't."

I nodded. "Shouldn't I be wrapped or taped?"

"Don't do that anymore. Chance of pneumonia."

Patrick snorted, and his eyes opened. He stretched. "Ow. What's wrong with my wrists?"

"Sprained. We took x-rays while you slept." The doctor walked to his bed. "You're lucky it was just your wrists. It would have been much worse if you hadn't landed on someone."

Patrick looked around the curtained room. "Where am I? What happened?" His eyes widened. "Who'd I land on?"

"We'll talk about it when we get home. When will they be released?" Patty asked.

"No time like the present," the doctor said. "The police were waiting to speak with you, but I put them off. I'm sure they'll be on your doorstep first thing tomorrow."

✷ ✷ ✷

James came to the garage to help me out of the car. Patrick insisted he could manage on his own. We walked into the house, and Jenny flew at me. Patty stepped in front of her. "Cracked rib, go easy on your mom."

Jenny embraced me gently.

Cindy said, "Where did you go? You said you'd only be gone a few minutes. We finished the movie and started to worry. Then Uncle James showed up and said Dad and Ms. March were in the hospital."

"Couch," I said, "and ice. Better bring some for Patrick's wrists too."

Matilda walked into the living room. "I waited. I wasn't sure what was going on, but I didn't want to leave till you got home. I'll get the ice."

Everyone sat. Matilda returned and handed an ice pack to me and two to Patrick. I told her, "Please sit. You may as well hear this at the same time as everyone else."

I nodded to Patrick, "You start. I'll finish the story."

When we were done, Patty clasped her hand over her mouth. I gave her a sharp look. "What?"

"When we were picking out a casket, Katie's arm looked like it had been burned. After Cindy got the same burn from breaking the oleander bush going after the football, I should have put it together. Katie must have avoided the cameras in the front and the garage by squeezing through the bushes on her way to kill Helen. Remember how Phillipe showed us the broken branch."

Patrick nodded. "She said it was sunburn."

"It wasn't. We'll need to lay it all out for the police when they come tomorrow. We should probably get some sleep."

James stood, his face stark white. "I want you to know I would never have given her any money. I can't believe she thought I would go along with this, that I cared so little about you." He hugged Patrick. "Please, believe me, bro. I want to have a lot more years of getting to know you." The door shut behind him.

I struggled to stand, and Jenny came to my aid. Patrick looked away. "I can't believe I landed on you. You're so little; you could have been smushed."

I laughed and clutched my ribs. "What makes you think I wasn't squashed?"

"I'm so sorry. Do you need help up the stairs?"

"I can do it. You need to rest your wrists." Jenny held out her arm, and Jenny and I made our way slowly up the stairs.

Cindy, Patty, and Patrick followed us.

"I'm glad you're okay, Dad." Cindy hugged him.

Patty put her arms around Patrick and kissed him. "I'm glad you're still here too. Now let's go to bed."

CHAPTER 31

Merry

I sat in the shower while Jenny used the handheld attachment to wash my hair. She finished, wrapped my hair in a towel, and said, "I'm glad I changed into my bathing suit, I'm getting wet. Do you think you can do everything else?"

"I've got it, thanks."

She left.

Somehow I managed to get the rest of me clean and toweled dry. I took another towel, draped it across my pillow, and lay down. I groaned. This was not going to work. I piled pillows behind me and sank onto the bed. That was much better. I slept.

My phone buzzed from the other side of the room at five in the morning. I groaned, stood, and shuffled to the dresser. *Who on earth is calling so early?* It was Father Tom. "Hello?"

"Merry, I've been trying to reach you."

I groaned as I sat on the bed, and my pain level spiked. "Sorry. Yesterday was a busy day."

"I have good news for you."

"I could use some of that. What is it?" I leaned back on the pillow fort I had built. It was better.

"Your annulment was approved. I should get the paperwork back in a few days, but I wanted to let you know right away."

"That's great, Father."

"You don't sound very enthusiastic."

"I am. It's just that it's five in the morning here." I coughed and then clutched my ribs.

"My apologies. Andy told me you were in Phoenix. I forgot about the time difference."

"No problem. I'll be home in a few days, so I'll schedule some time with you. I am quite pleased."

"I'll see you then."

I pressed end and tried to get comfortable. It wasn't going to happen, so I got up and, with some wrangling, was able to get dressed. My hair was a mess after sleeping on it wet, but there wasn't much I was going to be able to do about that.

I tiptoed down the stairs and into the kitchen. Matilda had just started the coffee. I lowered myself onto a stool. "You're here early this morning."

"I thought I'd make pastries and eggs benedict this morning to celebrate." She smiled. "I feel like a big weight has been lifted from my shoulders."

"Sounds delicious. Do you have any over the counter pain relievers? I don't want to take the heavy stuff they gave me."

"I'm sorry. Here I am jabbering away." She opened a drawer, took out a bottle, shook two pills into my hand, and gave me a glass of water. "Why don't you sit in the living room, and I'll bring coffee as soon as it's ready."

"Thanks." I popped the pills in my mouth and swallowed. Then I wandered into the living room and dropped down on the recliner. It was mechanical, so all I had to do was push a button, and it gently moved backward. There, that was almost comfortable. I shut my eyes.

"Mom, mom. Are you okay?" A hand shook my shoulder.

I stretched and screamed. "Ow, ow, ow. I can't do that."

Jenny's worried face stared down at me. "Why are you sleeping in the living room, and what happened to your hair?"

I felt my hair and groaned. "I know it's a mess."

"I'll be right back."

My eyes shut, and the doorbell rang. As I pressed the button to move the recliner into an upright position, Matilda ran by. "I'll get it."

Jenny clomped down the steps, brush in hand. She started detangling my hair as Lieutenant Muniz, and Detective Schwartz rounded the corner.

The lieutenant said, "Sorry to bother you so early. We're holding Katie Glass at the station and need to get more information. Are you two the only ones up?"

Patty and Patrick walked down the stairs. "We're up."

They sat on the sofa. Patty's eyebrow spiked as she looked at me. "Nice hair."

Jenny continued brushing. "It's better, but I'll need to put water on it to flatten the parts that are sticking up."

I took the brush, and she sat on the arm of the chair.

Matilda asked, "Would anyone like coffee?"

The lieutenant and detective nodded in unison. Patty rose. "I'll help."

Soon everyone had coffee, and a platter of freshly-baked Danish pastries graced the table.

Lieutenant Muniz turned toward Patrick. "So, Katie Glass lured you to the Outlook with the intent of causing your death?"

Patty nodded. "That's what she told Merry and me. Patrick was asleep when she admitted it. She also told us she smothered Helen with a pillow."

Patrick and Patty took turns explaining what happened in greater detail, and I chimed in occasionally.

The lieutenant and detective rose. Detective Schwartz said, "I'd appreciate it if you would stop by the office later today to sign your statements. After that, you're free to return home. I have your cell numbers if I have more questions."

The lieutenant eyed the Danish. "Any chance we could get some of that to-go?"

Matilda laughed and handed them a box she'd already prepared. They left. Then she asked, "Who's up for eggs benedict?"

* * *

The rest of the day was a flurry of booking flights, packing, and a last trip to the police station to sign our statements. Then, Patty took an Uber to the Outlook so she could bring back Patrick's rental. At least Louisa had done the laundry, so everything in our suitcases was clean. I mostly watched the action from the recliner, and every hour someone handed me an ice pack. Later in the afternoon, after carefully putting Patrick's mother's urn in her carry-on, Patty collapsed on the sofa next to me. "Will you be happy to go home tomorrow?"

"I'll regret leaving this lap of luxury, but I'll be happy to see the cats. And, Rob."

She smiled. "I don't know how we're going to thank you for coming here."

"We're friends. That's what we do."

"Have you forgiven Patrick for falling on you?" Her foot nudged mine.

"Barely."

"He bought us seats in first class for the trip home."

"I guess I can forgive him." I chuckled. "Oh, I forgot to tell you."

"What?"

"My annulment came through."

"Hallelujah! Matilda's making a chateaubriand for our last night, and this gives us another reason to celebrate. Have you told Jenny yet? Rob must be over the moon."

"I haven't told them yet. I just told you."

She frowned. "What's wrong? You're not feeling bad about cutting the final tie to that loser, Drew, are you?"

"I'd have to be a robot not to feel anything. He and I had Jenny together, and I'll always cherish that. As for the rest," a grin spread across my face, "I'm ecstatic."

Jenny walked in. "What are you so happy about?"

All of my muscles tightened, and my face fell. "My annulment to your father was finalized."

"That's great. Now you and he can move on." She sat on the arm of the chair and kissed my head. "I am happy for both you and Dad, Mom."

I relaxed. "Thanks, sweetie."

"What did Rob say? Was he happy?"

"I'll let him know right now." My fingers flew across the screen: "Annulment finalized. Happy days."

Jenny tapped my shoulder. "I can't believe you texted instead of calling him."

"Just wait." I smiled as my phone rang. "Hello, Rob."

ABOUT THE AUTHOR

Eileen Curley Hammond is an author who retired from a successful marketing career in the insurance industry. She and her husband share the house with two cats that are having a hard time training them.

For those of you who have been keeping up on this page, you know that Eileen and her husband restocked the fish pond last year with koi, shubunkins, and minnows. They are happily swimming in peace with screens and motion sensors guarding their kingdom.

The author looks forward to continuing to write and to the end of this pandemic. Stay safe, everyone.

www.ingramcontent.com/pod-product-compliance
Lightning Source LLC
Chambersburg PA
CBHW022109240626
47153CB00007B/2295